OPERATION R.A.D.

MAYA AHMED

HEMBURY BOOKS

First published by Hembury Books in 2026
hemburybooks.com.au
info@hemburybooks.com

Paperback ISBN 9781923517660
Ebook ISBN 9781923517653

This is a work of fiction. Names, characters, places, events, and incidents are products from the author's imagination. Any resemblance to anyone living, dead, fictional or events is purely coincidental.

This book contains mild coarse language, depictions of bullying, and emotional distress relevant to the plot and character development. These elements are included for dramatic and narrative purposes only. They are not intended to promote harmful behaviour. The characters' thoughts, dialogue, actions and behaviour are fictional and do not reflect the beliefs, attitude or behaviour of the author.

A catalogue record for this book is available from the National Library of Australia

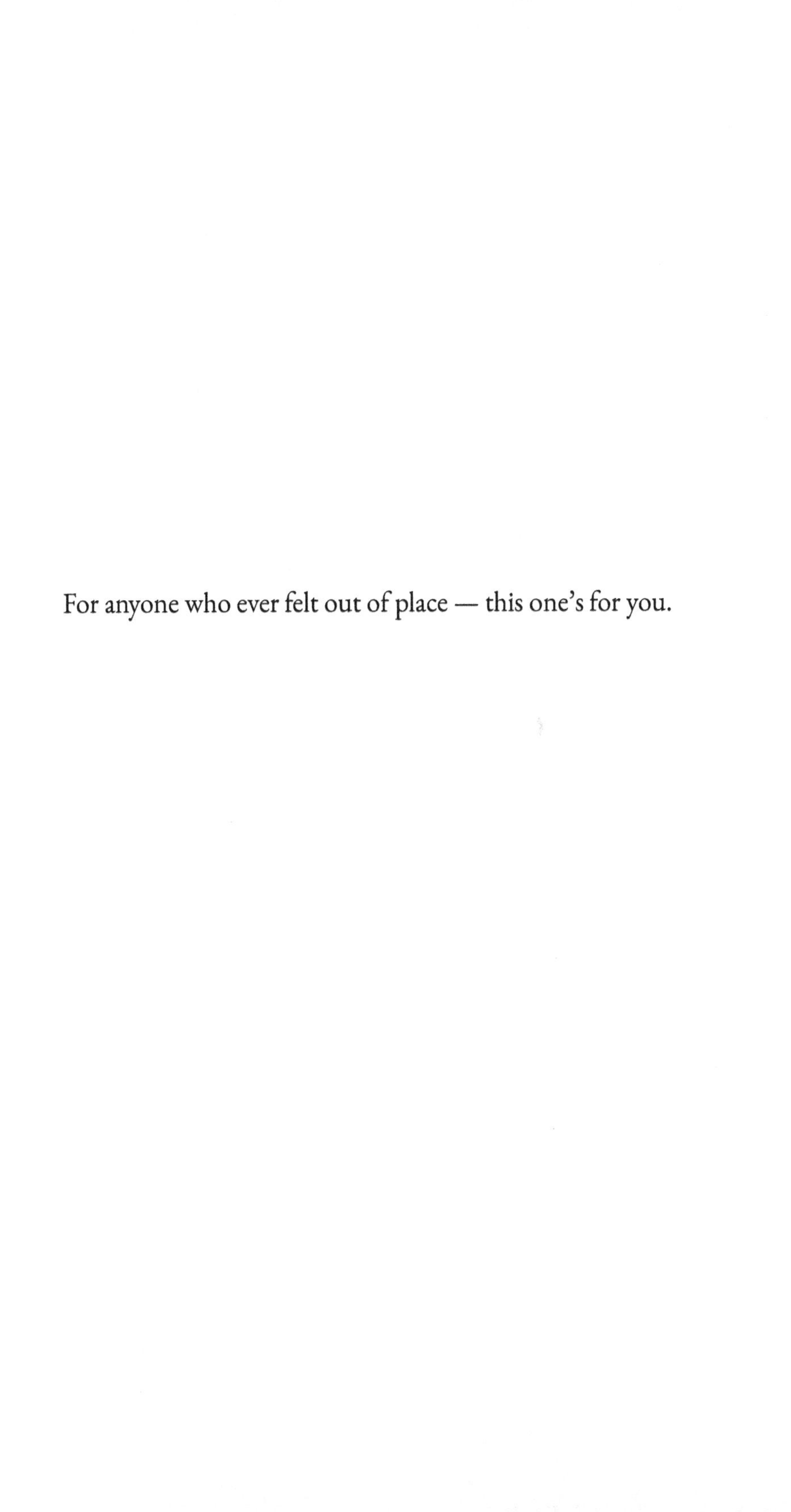

For anyone who ever felt out of place — this one's for you.

'If you've ever felt like you don't fit in, you were never meant to.'
— Maya Ahmed

Pinterest page
Fan art, early news, and other fans!
www.pinterest.com/maabooks2025

About the author

Maya Ariana Ahmed is a thirteen-year-old girl from Sydney, Australia. Since she was eleven, she has been fascinated by the generations before her, especially the 1980s and 1990s. She loves everything about those decades: the style, the shows, the slang and the music.

She has always been an enthusiastic reader of science fiction and mystery novels and often borrows books from her school library. The first series she read was *Renegades* by Marissa Meyer, and she has also read *The Mayfair Mysteries* by Alex Carter.

Maya took her passion for science fiction and wrote her first novella, *The Purple Demon (Dark Origins)*, when she was just twelve. Later that same year, she completed its sequel, *The Purple Demon II (New Lives and Family Ties)*.

Inspired by her love for the genre, Maya went on to write *Operation R.A.D.*, her first full-length novel. The story blends mystery, adventure and heart, capturing the wild energy of retro movies, neon lights and the chaos of being a teenager trying to do the right thing in a world that rarely makes sense.

Table of Contents

Playlist

Chapter 1
Time After Time – Cyndi Lauper

Chapter 2
Under Pressure – Queen and David Bowie

Chapter 3
Hit Me with Your Best Shot – Pat Benatar

Chapter 4
Love is a Battlefield – Pat Benatar

Chapter 5
Drive – The Cars

Chapter 6
Against All Odds – Phil Collins

Chapter 7
Walking on Sunshine – Katrina and the Waves

Chapter 8
You Spin Me Round (Like a Record) – Dead or Alive
Footloose – Kenny Loggins
Let's Go Crazy – Prince
P.Y.T – Micheal Jackson
Girls Just Wanna Have Fun – Cyndi Lauper
Conga – Gloria Estefan

Chapter 1

Addison: Big Changes

It was supposed to be a normal Sunday afternoon with my friends at our favourite pizza shop in Clearridge. The Saucy Slide. Until Mum found out that she got promoted, and with that promotion, came a new town.

Ravenwood.

Me and my mum were packing the last bags into the car, and I was clearly mad the entire time we were packing our things and selling the house.

"Addison, I know you don't want to leave Clearridge, but don't make this harder for me than it already is," said my mum with an annoyed expression.

"Well, it's not my fault that I don't want to leave my hometown," I snapped back. My arms were crossed so tight my chest hurt.

My mum aggressively slammed a box into the boot of the car. "Addison, stop giving me attitude. We are moving to Ravenwood."

I scoffed and rolled my eyes. "It sounds like the kind of place where a horror movie starts."

"Addison Taylor Moore!" yelled my mum as she slammed the boot shut.

I jumped, not because of her yelling, but because I like my fingers attached. She rolled her eyes and got into the car, and I reluctantly followed.

I turned around to look at Clearridge one last time. My home, my friends, my entire life. Every good memory hit me at once, and suddenly I couldn't see through the tears. I waved goodbye to my best friends, Jessica, Katie and Jenny, who all looked like they were going to cry.

"Wait!" yelled Jessica.

I got out of the car to see what happened.

"This is so you never forget us," said Katie, holding out a silver locket.

"Please don't forget us," said Jenny.

"Never," I said as we all had a group hug.

Jessica put the locket around my neck and secured it. She smoothed my hair like she always did when I was about to cry. I opened the locket, and it revealed a photo of Jenny, Jessica, Katie and me. I tried not to cry as I got back into the car and waved goodbye.

I turned to my mum to see if she was sad, but surprise, surprise, she was not even a little bit sad. If anything, she was happy that we were moving out of Clearridge. The car started abruptly, and we set of for Ravenwood.

"Mum?" I asked quietly.

"What?" she snapped, annoyed that I was even talking.

"Are you upset that we're leaving?"

"Not really. Clearridge was a pretty basic town."

I gaped at her as my fingers gripped the box next to me, my knuckles turning white. I turned away from her to avoid showing her how truly hurt I was. She always told me that 'emotions were for the weak.' I didn't believe that.

I closed my eyes, trying to think of one thing, anything, to make me feel safe, but there was nothing. I was leaving my life behind, my mum doesn't care how I feel, and I have no friends. My throat tightened and I bit the inside of my cheek to stop the tears.

Soon enough I actually fell asleep, and I slept for two hours. Suddenly there was a pothole, and I bounced up from my seat abruptly. Now that

I was awake there was no hope of me going back to sleep. I kept shifting in my seat trying to make myself comfortable, but when you're sitting between a giant box of fragile cutlery and an even bigger box of even more fragile plates you have no hope of being comfortable.

After three long hours of driving to this mysterious Ravenwood, we were finally there. The place looked dead and the only people who were out were old people feeding ducks and pigeons at the park. The town square had a fountain that was supposed to be fancy, but the water was shut off, and a bunch of overgrown weeds had made that their new home. My mum drove for another five minutes. That's when we finally made it to the place I had to call home.

It was a small, two-storey house with old, chipped black and grey paint and broken windows. The garden consisted mostly of dead plants, except for a small rose bush. A girl who looked around my age was tending to it. As soon as she saw the car pull in, she bolted the opposite way and disappeared into the unsettling forest behind the house.

My mum and I got out of the car, and I walked towards the rose bush. There was an envelope attached to it. I grabbed it and ripped it open. The note said

Welcome to Ravenwood, I hope you like the flowers.
– J. P.

"Addison, hurry up and help me with the boxes!" shouted my mum. "Coming," I said, as I held the note and looked back into the forest with some hope of finding the girl.

I went to the car and helped my mum bring in a box of photo albums. I stepped into the old house, and it was the dustiest place I had ever been in. I made a disgusted face.

"You'll get used to it," said my mum, without me even saying anything.

The silence in the new house was unnerving. Back in Clearridge you would always hear the birds chirping happily and the kids playing in the playground down the street. I set the box down on the grimy, cracked kitchen counter and looked around.

The bottom floor had a small kitchen, an even smaller living room and a tiny bathroom. The second floor had two small bedrooms and a bathroom the size of a closet.

I noticed sticky green goo dripping from the smaller bedroom's air conditioner. I grimaced at the acrid smell, but felt weirdly attracted to it. My hand reached out to touch it.

Suddenly my mum shouted, "Addison, you get the smaller room, go put all your stuff there!"

I pulled myself away from the green goo and scurried down the stairs. I grabbed my box. It had my boom box, posters, clothes, shoes and toiletries. I started to put everything away and hung my Madonna and Prince posters up on the walls. Once mum started giving me my allowance, I was definitely going to buy some paint and wood for shelves.

"Addison, dinner's ready," said my mum.

I went downstairs to the dining table and saw a box of greasy pizza on the table. My mum was there too.

I gaped at the oily monstrosity sitting on the table. I could swear the pizza was melting the box at this point.

"I know it's not like the one in Clearridge, but it's the only pizza place Ravenwood's got," said my mum.

I sat down, disgusted by how much oil was on the pizza, and that's when I did the thing I regretted the most. I took a slice and bit into it. It was rubbery and disgustingly oily. I excused myself and went to the bathroom, where I spat out the pizza and rinsed my mouth, but the water from the sink tasted bitter and metallic, leaving a chalky film on my tongue. I gagged as the stale, muddy flavour lingered in my mouth.

I was about to throw up. "Mum? Do we have any water?"

"Yeah, it's in the fridge."

She didn't even look up from her work papers. It was probably a good thing, otherwise she would have seen my disgusted face and yelled at me about 'not being grateful'.

I gulped down the bottle of water.

"By the way, Addison don't drink from the tap. It's not clean."

"Obviously," I muttered to myself as I rolled my eyes.

I went to my room and got ready for bed. I thought about everything that happened today. Moving cities, leaving my friends, the weird green goo, the disgusting oily pizza and the locket. I took it off and left it on top of one of my boxes as I lay down on my bed, which was a half blown up mattress. I was still hungry, but there was no way I was going to eat pizza or any oily food from this place ever again. I closed my eyes and hoped that school would make this town ten times better.

It was the morning of the worst day of my life, and I didn't even know it. It was the first day of high school at Ravenwood high. I was so excited, I hoped this would make up for having such a bad house and shitty food. It was hard to sleep at night in my new bed (mattress). I wasn't sure if it was being away from home or if the mattress was just uncomfortable.

I got up at five a.m. and I actually did my make-up. My mum never showed me how to, but luckily Jessica had. I straightened my hair, because it looks like a mess when I don't, and I wanted to make a good first impression. I wore my favourite pink mini skirt, a white shirt, and my Buster Browns to stay comfy, but I forgot to wear any jewellery other than my locket. Big mistake.

I walked up to the school bus excitedly, eager to make new friends. The bus was painted in shades of grey and it looked intimidating, but I was sure I would get used to it. I stepped up to the heavy grey door and pressed a big red button. The door opened and I got in. As soon as I walked in everyone stared at me, and not in a good way. I still walked with my head high anyway. One girl gave me dirty looks and others whispered to each other and snickered as I shuffled past them. I was worried that people thought I was a joke or a misfit. It hurt, and my shoulders slumped. I thought this was going to be a fresh start for me. To actually make friends, I needed this school to work, otherwise I'll have to spend the next four years as an outsider in this town. I sat in a spot by myself.

I unhooked the locket from its chain to remind me of my old friends. I really wished they were here. They would have comforted me and looked after me. I held the locket in my left hand. That's when I realised the green goo from the air conditioner had gotten on it. I quickly wiped it off with my finger before it stained the locket, but when I opened it, instead of seeing me and my three best friends, there were two. Katie had disappeared.

'Okay. Weird. Totally normal. Maybe the glue lifted. Maybe the photo folded. Maybe Ravenwood air eats pictures.'

I clicked it shut and tucked it under my shirt, my heart hammering.

I tried not to stare at anyone, but I couldn't help it. People-watching is what I do when I'm bored.

A boy two rows up was doodling in the margins of his notebook, blowing a strand of hair out of his face over and over. A kid near the front had a stack of textbooks so high I couldn't even see his eyes. Another girl had a clover choker that flashed when she laughed too loud. Across the aisle, one girl sat hunched over, turning a bracelet around on her wrist like she was trying to calm herself down, while the boy behind her flicked open a Rubik's Cube and twisted it, not looking up. Just more faces in the blur. Everyone else blended into greys and blues and acid-wash.

Suddenly the bus braked and we were at school. I waited until it emptied. When I stood, the girl with the clover choker clipped my shoulder with her bag. She rolled her eyes at me.

I went to the front office. The lady sitting there had a neat bun.

"Hi, I'm Addison Moore. I'm in Year 9."

The woman smiled warmly. "Hi, Addison, I'm Mrs Serenity. I just need your birthday and then I can give you your locker and timetable."

"Yep, it's the twenty-second of September 1969," I said. She gave me a piece of paper that said Locker 313 and my timetable.

'Maths. First period. Seriously?'

I looked for my locker and there it was. Number 313. It was in a shady part at the back of the school. There were no other lockers there, just giant rubbish bins and bushes that looked like they hadn't been trimmed in over twenty years. The whole area made me feel uncomfortable, like someone was going to come out of those bushes and grab me. I put my stuff away and went to my Maths class.

I sat in a seat not too close to the front and not too close to the back, because I didn't want people to think I was a dork, and I didn't want teachers to think that I was a bad student. Even though I might be.

"What do you think you're doing?" asked the girl with the clover choker who had rolled her eyes at me. She was blonde, light skinned, had a fluffy side ponytail and a choker with a four-leaf clover on it. I read about four-leaf clovers, and they're supposed to bring good luck. Her hoop earrings were so big they could've picked up TV signals, and her scrunchies were brighter than highlighters. From her tone I could tell she was the 'queen bee' around here, and she was about to make my school life a living hell, but I didn't want her to know that I knew that.

"Sitting," I replied with my head high.

I thought that would show her that she didn't intimidate me, but it didn't. The girl rolled her eyes and scoffed

"Well, I'm Blaire, I'm the queen bee, my dad is the richest man in town and this is my seat, got it? Go sit at the front with the dorks or something, I don't really care."

By then three girls were behind her, giving me death glares. So, I reluctantly grabbed my things and got up. She gave me a 'that's what I thought smirk'.

I wished I had punched her plastic nose.

As I went to sit near the front like she told me to, I saw her and her friends looking at me. They were snickering and whispering. Then my worst nightmare happened. The teacher finally arrived. He looked crazy and dishevelled, but he didn't say anything to Blaire and her friends who were talking. Instead, he did the thing that no person should ever deal with on their first day of school. He pointed at me.

"You're the new girl, right?"

"Yep, that's me!" I replied cheerfully trying to hide how pissed off I was.

"Come on up here and introduce yourself."

I froze. I was never good at public speaking. In fact, it was one of my worst fears. With shaking legs, I stood up and went to the front of the class.

"Hi, I'm Addison and..."

I was interrupted by Blaire.

"She wore those shoes? Gag me with a spoon!" said Blaire, laughing as loudly as possible.

Then the entire class erupted with laughter. I wished I could've dissolved into the ground at that moment.

"Seriously, Addi, did your grandma dress you?" said Blaire, rocking on her chair. I hoped it would fall over backwards with her on it.

But then I looked at my shoes like really looked at them and thought,

'What's wrong with them?'

Everyone went silent and stared at me. Blaire looked shocked.

"What?" I asked.

That's when I realised that I wasn't thinking it —I actually said it. The silence hit like someone had dropped the boom box cord at a party. Even Blaire looked thrown for a second before her glare locked on me like a laser.

"Okay everyone, today we will continue learning about exponents,." said the teacher, trying to break the awkward silence. I sat down and I could still feel Blaire glaring at me the entire lesson.

Chapter 2

Julianna: Holding On

It was time to come back to school at Ravenwood High, and I wished I didn't have to. I had just gotten back from the Cerulia islands, where me, my mum and dad, my brothers, Kai and Jaxon, and my sisters, Lyra and Kaelin, go every year. I wish those days never ended. At the Cerulia islands, the sun was always out, and no one made you feel bad or worthless. Unlike Ravenwood High, where if you even sneeze someone will find a way to make fun of you.

I was in my room picking out an outfit for my first day of school. Year 9 was going to be tough. Especially with those 'social predators.' Every time I walk into a room with them, I don't feel safe. They could do anything to me and no one would even try to stop them. While I was thinking, I didn't realise that I had my hair straightener on one part of my hair for way too long and it burned a bit of my hair.

"Shit," I whispered.

I quickly tried to hide that part of my hair under more hair. That's when I checked the time and realised I was going to miss the bus.

I slipped on my favourite blue t-shirt, dark blue jeans and my red Converse. Just before I left, I grabbed my ocean bracelet. My grandmother had made it for me on my sixth birthday, and I took it with me wherever I went. It made me feel safe. Whenever I didn't feel safe, I held on to the bracelet, hoping it would save me.

That's when I realised there was something green and gooey on it. It looked like slime. Sighing, I thought to myself,

'Lyra must have gotten her slime on it.'

"Julianna, you're going to be late," said my mum.

I sprinted down the stairs, and quickly grabbed my bag, my book and stuffed a piece of toast into my mouth.

"Bye mum," I said with my mouth full. I swallowed the bread and just made it onto the bus in time, and that's when I saw her.

Blaire Pembroke. She thinks she's so much better than everyone else because her dad is rich. She always bullies me and my best friend, Ivory. She's the reason I hate school. She's the social predator. Whenever she was around, I tried to lay low, covering my face with my book or my hair and slouching, hoping she wouldn't notice I was there.

"Hey dork," said Blaire, smirking, with her minions behind her.

"Oh h-h-hi Blaire," I said, smiling, though deep down I hated her more than anything, but I couldn't say anything because my parents work for her dad, and my parents need their jobs.

"How are you?" I asked still smiling.

"Do you ever shut up, Julianna? Not everything needs care bears and rainbows."

At that exact moment all my friends all got on the bus. Ivory, Mateo, Avery and Randy. They all looked pissed off. Except for Randy, he didn't really care about anything besides his Rubik's Cube.

Blaire walked to the back with her minions, snickering, and then I heard her say something that made my stomach drop.

"She's so energetic, even her shadow looks like it had too much cola."

"Don't let her get to you," said Ivory, sitting down next to me. She put her arm around me, and it made me feel a bit better. I swallowed hard and nodded.

"It's okay, maybe she's just having a bad day."

"Girl, if that's her bad day then she has the worst day every day," said Ivory.

"Yeah, true."

"Anyway, I've got to get some homework done. Who does Mrs Lindsey think she is, giving us holiday homework!?"

I laughed.

I rested my head on the window while she did her homework. I wished I could be on the beach, surfing and swimming and just being near water. I wished I could ride the waves right now instead of riding the bus with Blaire. I pulled out my book from my bag. It was called *The Adventures of Cascade*. It was about a girl who spent so much time near the water that they became connected, and she could control the water with a flick of her wrist. I wished I could have water powers. My friends and I could build our own pool, and I could fill it. My family wouldn't have to pay the water bill, and we could save money. I was going to be fifteen- and nine-months next year, which meant I could finally help out by getting a job, and I wanted to be a lifeguard. Being around water all day after school and getting paid for it would be perfect. Then Blaire came back. Of course she did.

"Whatcha reading, dork?" asked Blaire as she snatched my book.

"Blaire, please give it back," I asked as I tried to grab the book back. Everyone was looking at us and I felt nervous. I rubbed my hand over my bracelet, hoping it would protect me, but it never did around Blaire.

"What a dumb book," said Blaire as she flipped through the pages.

"Maybe 'cause you're holding the book upside down," said Mateo, not looking up from his History homework.

"Excuse me?" said Blaire.

"You heard me," said Mateo, staring at Blaire with no emotion. Which somehow made him look intimidating.

Blaire rolled her eyes. "Whatever. You're all, like... totally bogus anyway." Then she looked back at me. "Julianna, you're like... a confused toaster. Always popping up when no one's hungry."

'What does that even mean?' I thought to myself.

Everyone just looked at Blaire, confused, except for her minions, Clarissa, Geniessa and Larissa, who started cackling like that was the funniest thing in the world. She walked to the back of the bus.

Mateo turned to me. "Just ignore her, Jules."

"Yeah, she's just a dumb b..." started Ivory as the bus suddenly braked. Blaire, who had been standing up, went flying forward. She caught herself on a seat before hitting the ground. No one laughed, even though it was probably the funniest thing that had ever happened in Ravenwood High.

Randy looked up from his Rubik's Cube. "We don't usually stop here."

Ivory looked around. "Maybe there's a new student."

"I hope they're not like Blaire," Avery muttered under his breath.

A girl with straight dark brown hair and beautiful wide eyes of the same shade stepped onto the bus. She didn't look like she belonged to the same world as the rest of us. While everyone else faded into the dull greys and blues of bleached jeans and t-shirts, she was a burst of neon against the gloom. Her bright pink mini skirt demanded attention, swinging with every step, and her worn-out Buster Browns made a sharp statement of their own. Old-fashioned, definitely out of place, but she wore it with so much confidence that they looked intentional. Conversations dipped for a moment as people glanced her way, some whispering, some staring. She wasn't trying to fit in. She didn't need to. Then her shoulders slumped a little. I noticed Blaire and her friends snickering at the back.

"Blaire is such a..." said Ivory, who was interrupted by Avery.

"Why can't Blaire ever shut up?"

We all shrugged.

"Poor girl, she's sitting by herself," I said.

"It's okay Jules," said Ivory, giving my shoulders a squeeze. "Watch, once we get to school, she's going to have so many friends."

I smiled even though I knew that was not happening. Blaire was going to make this girl her target, which meant no one would try to be friends with her.

"When we get to school, I'm going to talk to her," I said.

"Okay, just be careful Blaire doesn't try anything," said Ivory.

When we finally got to school the new girl disappeared in the crowd of five hundred teenagers in the hallway.

"It's okay, we'll find her after class," said Ivory.

"Yeah, what class do we have?" I asked.

"Maths. Let's just make sure we don't sit in 'Blaire's seat'," said Ivory, doing air quotes.

We both laughed and made our way to our Maths class. We sat down, I kept reading and Ivory kept doing her homework.

"Ivory, look, it's the new girl!" I said, standing up.

Ivory turned around and then tugged at my shirt. I stopped out of curiosity.

"She's sitting in Blaire's seat. Trouble is coming."

Right at that moment Blaire came and started giving the girl a hard time. I felt bad, but there was nothing I could do. I sat back down and slumped in my seat. Ivory put her hand on my shoulder. "It's not your fault."

I gave her a small, forced smile.

Suddenly the door flew open and Mr Bentley ran in, coffee stains on his shirt and a messy pile of papers in his hands, as usual. Then he did the thing that no one should have to deal with on their first day of high school. He pointed at the new girl and told her to introduce herself to the class.

The girl got up and went to the front of the classroom. She looked nervous and I felt bad for her.

"Hi, I'm Addison and..." She was interrupted by Blaire.

"She wore those shoes? Gag me with a spoon!" said Blaire, laughing as loud as possible. Then the entire class erupted with laughter. But not real laughter. They only laughed so they wouldn't be Blaire's victims. I wanted to say something, but I just couldn't.

"Seriously, Addi, did your grandma dress you?" said Blaire, leaning back on her chair.

I could see tears in Addison's eyes, and then just pure confusion. Then she made the worst mistake anyone could ever make. She asked, "What's wrong with them?"

Everyone went silent and stared at her. Blaire looked shocked.

"What?" asked Addison.

Blaire stared at her. We all knew she would be her next victim.

"Okay everyone, today we will continue learning about exponents," said Mr Bentley.

Chapter 3

Addison: Keep it Together

It was 11:20 a.m. History. The class that would make or break my future, and I didn't even know it. Today was crazy. Being the new girl in a pink mini skirt and Buster Browns was the worst decision I could ever make. It was just before lunch, and my stomach was eating itself. I hadn't eaten since yesterday morning. The classroom was on the third floor, in the corner of the level. I had to take six flights of stairs to get up there and my legs were burning by the time I got to the classroom. Once inside, I noticed something was off. The lights kept flickering, but weirdly. Like it was a heartbeat. Somehow no one else seemed to notice, but I couldn't take my eyes off it.

"Hello everyone! I am Mrs Lindsey."

She looked very sweet, but I soon realised I was very *very* wrong.

"For your assessment task in a few weeks you'll need a team, and since the last class didn't go well with choosing groups, *I* will put you into groups of eight."

"Okay, group one: Bella Anderson, Anthony Cuff, Elizabeth Green, Rebecca Han, Tina Klan, Andy Lorn and Omar Mcphoon."

They all looked happy to be in the same group.

"Group two: Orion Black, Larissa Blane, Jesse G, Clarissa Gold, Alya James, Tim Lee, Geniessa Stone and Mark Walker."

A boy kicked a chair and it flew to the other side of the room, nearly knocking two girls' heads off. Then two boys got up and grabbed the chair and threw it at the boy who'd kicked it.

"Boys! No throwing or kicking!" yelled Mrs Lindsey.

The two boys sat down.

'Great. If this is what class is going to be like, then I'll probably end up being a victim on the second day.'

Mrs Lindsey rolled her eyes. "Group three: Blake Armstrong, Randy Ford, Julianna Kim, Addison Moore, Avery Pearce, Ivory Pearce, Blaire Pembroke and Mateo Ramirez."

My blood ran cold. Blaire and I were in the same group and those words kept repeating themselves over and over in my mind.

Suddenly I heard someone say, "Who's Addison?"

It was a boy with dark brown curls that stuck out in different directions, never quite staying down. His tan skin contrasted with the bright red of his shirt, and his blue jeans were creased like he'd been wearing them every day.

"That girl over there," said a girl. Her hair was straight, black and she had a fringe; she looked like she'd stepped out of a magazine. Her little ocean charms on her bracelet caught the light, swaying every time she moved. Cute, but somehow mysterious.

The group walked up to me and the girl with the black hair said, "Hi! I'm Julianna, but my friends call me Jules and so can you!"

"Hi," I said.

"Let's introduce ourselves," said Julianna.

"Hi, I'm Mateo," said the guy with the curly hair.

"I'm Randy," said a boy.

He had light brown hair neatly combed, pale skin, and glasses that slid down his nose just enough to make him look thoughtful. Denim jacket over denim jeans. It was a lot of denim, but somehow it suited him, like he belonged more in a corner with a book than the chaos in our classroom with Blaire and the chair-kicking guy.

"That's Ivory and Avery; they don't talk that much," said Julianna as she pointed at a girl and a boy.

The girl was tiny, skinny and short, with silky black hair that fell over one side of her face, hiding her left eye. Light skin, a simple green shirt, and a little flower necklace. There was something delicate about her, like she could disappear if you weren't looking closely.

The boy had pale skin and black hair falling over one eye, giving him that half-hidden look, like he didn't want to be seen. Leather jacket, fingerless gloves. Everything about him screamed edge, like danger wrapped in quiet cool.

"You've already met Blaire, and that's Blake," said Julianna as she pointed at a tall guy with blond permed hair. He was discreetly playing on his Game & Watch.

"Sup, losers?" said Blaire. "Seriously, you didn't even wear any jewellery. Are you poor or something?" Blaire laughed. Only this time no one was laughing because the only people who heard were in our group, and they were all really nice. I'm not sure about Blake; he still looked distracted playing on his Game & Watch. "What are we doing for the project?" asked Mateo.

"Mrs Lindsey hasn't told us yet. I think she'll tell us closer to the actual date," replied Julianna.

Suddenly the bell rang, and everyone sprinted to the cafeteria for lunch. The line was bigger than the line for a Disneyland roller coaster. Luckily, my mum had packed me lunch, so I didn't have to wait in line. The cafeteria food didn't look too good anyway. It was all disgustingly oily, which people in this town seemed to like for some reason. I walked over to an empty table near the side of the cafeteria. I unhooked my necklace again to see if I was just imagining Katie being replaced with a blur, but when I looked at it, Katie was still gone. My stomach growled. I took the sandwich out from its aluminium foil, but as I was about to take a bite, Blaire came and knocked it out of my hands.

"Go buy food like the rest of us, weirdo," said Blaire, laughing with her group, like they were her minions.

It was only the first day of school, but I was so sick of this. I stood up and slammed my hands on the table. The whole cafeteria went dead silent, and I saw Julianna jump from the other table.

"Back off Blaire!" I yelled, walking towards her.

She turned around and grinned.

"Bite me!" she spat, laughing.

I crossed my arms, "Seriously, Barbie called, she wants her wardrobe back."

I could feel everyone's eyes on us.

"Excuse me?" said Blaire in the most dramatic tone.

I smirked, "I'd say don't let your mouth write cheques your attitude can't cash... but you wouldn't get it."

"Ooh!" said everyone unison.

"Bite me!" she spat, laughing again.

Rolling my eyes, I thought to myself,

'She's like a cassette stuck on repeat, the same boring lines over and over.'

"Okay!" I said, a little too excited, I ran at Blaire, and she jumped to the side.

"I thought you wanted me to bite you. Queen bee's too scared, isn't she?" I said, mockingly.

"I'm not scared!" yelled Blaire defensively.

"Then fight me!" I roared.

She stepped back awkwardly, almost losing balance with her heels.

'Screw it' I thought, 'This girl needs to know what she just walked into.'

And with that I swung my fist.

Chapter 4

Ivory: One of Those Days

It was time for my least favourite subject: History. There was always something off about our teacher, Mrs Lindsey. Her smile was always a bit too wide for her face, and we didn't learn half the things that were in the exam, but this year something else was wrong. The lights. They kept flickering, but in a really odd way. As if they were blinking or trying to send a message. It made me feel uneasy.

My brother, Avery, was next to me as we shuffled to the back of the class. I tugged his sleeve, and he flinched.

"Sorry," I whispered.

"It's fine, you just scared me," Avery whispered back.

"Can you see it as well?" I asked, "With the lights."

He looked around. "Yeah, something's wrong."

He knew I had a bad feeling about Mrs Lindsey and I'm pretty sure he did too.

I sat next to Julianna. She was still looking at the new girl, and I could tell she wanted to make sure she was okay, but I was worried Blaire would hurt her. Julianna was always too sweet. Even when someone did something wrong, she'd just brush it off as 'they weren't feeling good.'

Randy, Mateo and Avery were sitting behind us.

"Guys, what's going on with the lights?" I asked.

"I'm not sure, but I also have a bad feeling about it," said Julianna.

Mateo looked up. "Yeah, it looks like it's possessed," he said.

Randy rolled his eyes. "You guys worry too much. It probably just needs maintenance."

He was the one I liked the least out of our friend group. He was always rude to everyone and whenever anyone was sad or hurt, he would just say that they're overreacting, and he was always such a buzzkill.

"Hello everyone! I am Mrs Lindsey." said Mrs Lindsey. "For your assessment task in a few weeks you'll need a team, and since the last class didn't go well with choosing groups, *I* will put you into groups of eight."

My stomach tightened. When teachers used that phrase, say adios to your luck.

"Okay, group one: Bella Anderson, Anthony Cuff, Elizabeth Green, Rebecca Han, Tina Klan, Andy Lorn and Omar Mcphoon." They got lucky. They were all best friends.

"Group two: Orion Black, Larissa Blane, Jesse G, Clarissa Gold, Alya James, Tim Lee, Geniessa Stone and Mark Walker." Blaire's whole group was in that group. Geniessa, Clarissa and Larissa. Which meant that she was going to be alone.

Suddenly, Orion kicked a chair. It came right at me and Julianna's heads. We ducked just in time. Avery and Mateo got up and grabbed the chair and threw it back at Orion, almost smashing it into his face.

"Boys! No throwing or kicking!" yelled Mrs Lindsey.

Avery and Mateo sat back down.

Mrs Lindsey rolled her eyes like managing a class was the hardest thing in the world.

"Group three: Blake Armstrong, Randy Ford, Julianna Kim, Addison Moore, Avery Pearce, Ivory Pearce, Blaire Pembroke and Mateo Ramirez."

I let out a sigh of relief. Our entire friend group was together. Even if Blaire was in it, it would be five against one. I turned around and saw Julianna. Her shoulders relaxed and she beamed. That's when I realised Addison was the new girl. I smiled at her and nudged her shoulder.

"See, now you can be friends with her."

Julianna let out a happy but quiet squeal. She did that whenever she was really happy and I found it really funny.

"Who's Addison?" asked Mateo.

"That girl over there," said Julianna, pointing at Addison.

We all walked over to her, except for Julianna. She practically flew there.

"Hi! I'm Julianna, but my friends call me Jules and so can you," said Julianna enthusiastically.

"Hi," said Addison. She looked a bit hesitant, like she was examining each one of us.

"Let's introduce ourselves," said Julianna excitedly. She was literally jumping at this point.

"Hi, I'm Mateo."

"I'm Randy."

"That's Ivory and Avery. They don't talk that much," said Julianna.

I was glad Julianna said that because I get really nervous around new people and sometimes I almost forget how to talk, and Avery just doesn't like talking to people. He's such an introvert.

"You've already met Blaire, and that's Blake," said Julianna, pointing at Blaire and Blake.

"Sup, losers?" said Blaire. "Seriously, you didn't even wear any jewellery. Are you poor or something?" Blaire laughed, but no one else did, because the only people who heard were in our group and we all hate Blaire.

"What are we doing for the project?" Mateo asked, completely ignoring Blaire.

"Mrs Lindsey hasn't told us yet. I think she'll tell us closer to the actual date," replied Julianna.

Suddenly the bell rang and everyone sprinted to the cafeteria for lunch. The line was long, as usual. Our group usually waited until it got smaller, but while we were waiting, we saw Blaire and Addison at the table next to ours. Addison had a homemade sandwich, and she was about to take a bite out of it. Which is the biggest mistake you could make on the first day of high school in Ravenwood while being on Blaire's bad side.

Blaire walked up to Addison and slapped her food out of her hands.

"Go buy food like the rest of us, weirdo," she said, laughing with her group of hyenas.

Addison stood up and slammed her hands on the table. Julianna jumped because of the noise.

"Back off, Blaire!" yelled Addison.

I clapped a hand over my mouth, Randy stopped looking at his Rubik's Cube (which happens once in a lifetime), Avery looked up from his sketchbook, Mateo ran his hands through his hair and Julianna buried her face in her hands, peeking between her fingers. We all knew this wasn't going to go down well.

Blaire turned around, grinning.

"Bite me!" she yelled back, laughing.

Julianna went pale. She must've been worried about Addison.

"Seriously, Barbie called. She wants her wardrobe back," said Addison.

The whole cafeteria went silent as we all stared at them.

"Damn," whispered someone behind me.

Julianna gripped onto the table. "Not again," I heard her whisper under her breath.

"Julianna, what's wrong?" I whispered, trying not to draw any attention to her. She hates that.

"Excuse me?" said Blaire.

"I'd say don't let your mouth write cheques your attitude can't cash… but you wouldn't get it."

"Ooh" said everyone in unison.

My jaw clenched.

'Addison's dead.'

"I'm fine. I just need some water," whispered Julianna as she massaged her temples. Her breathing turned quick and shallow as she stood up, still gripping the table like her life depended on it.

"Bite me!" Blaire yelled, laughing again.

"Do you want me to come with you?" I asked.

"Okay!" said Addison looking a bit too happy.

Addison ran at Blaire and Blaire jumped to the side.

"I thought you wanted me to bite you. Queen bee's too scared, isn't she?" said Addison mockingly.

Julianna let go of the table and her knees buckled. Her hands clutched its edge for support as Randy's Rubik's Cube slid onto the floor. Avery dropped his pencil and Mateo leaned forward instinctively, as if he wanted to catch her but didn't know how.

"I'm not scared!" yelled Blaire defensively.

"Julianna," I said, putting my hand on her shoulder. "Is something wrong?"

"Then fight me!" roared Addison.

Blaire stepped back, almost losing her balance on her Christian Dior heels. I stared at those shoes for more than a few seconds. At first glance they looked real, but then I recognised them as knockoffs from the nearby thrift store. You could tell they were fakes because the dye was uneven. I was confused, because her dad was the richest man in town. Why would she be buying fakes?

"I'm fine. The line's short, I'll go get some water," said Julianna shakily. She was still gripping onto the table. She took a few wobbly steps to the line.

Addison ran and punched Blaire in her plastic nose.

Julianna collapsed and passed out.

"JULIANNA!" I yelled, reaching for her. Randy crouched beside her. Avery grabbed a water bottle from his bag, and Mateo gently lifted her head.

Blaire and Addison got into a fight and Addison pulled Blaire's oversized Napier earring out of her left ear.

"AAAGGH!" screamed Blaire.

Chapter 5

Addison: Domino Effect

We got into a cat fight and without thinking I reached up and grabbed one of her oversized earrings out of her ear.

"AAAGGH!" screamed Blaire, clutching her ear, blood dripping from her ear onto her neck.

I stood there with her hoop in my clenched fist. I wasn't ashamed of what I'd done.

"You psycho!" Blaire spat.

She stared at me like she was going to kill me with her eyes. I paused mid-fight, eyes wide.

"Oh no," muttered Randy.

"She's out cold!" shouted Avery.

"Check her breathing!" yelled Mateo.

I blinked. Out cold? What? Blaire was still giving me death glares. She wasn't out cold. That's when I turned and saw what everyone was looking at.

Julianna.

She was on the floor, her skin was pale, and her lips had lost their colour. My chest tightened.

"Oh my god..." said someone.

"Is she...?" asked another.

"Julianna!" I yelled as I pushed past the crowd of people. Trays slammed against my body; I tripped over shoes and spilled drinks. I finally got to Julianna's side and dropped beside her.

"Someone get water!" I yelled.

"I've got it!" Avery fumbled with his bottle, twisting the cap so fast water splashed onto his jeans.

"Talk to her! Keep her awake!" Mateo urged.

Ivory whispered desperately, "Julianna... it's okay...we're right here... wake up..."

"Someone call the nurse!" yelled Mateo.

A couple of kids ran to the nurse's office. Randy checked Julianna's pulse, Avery splashed water on her face and Ivory shook her gently while yelling her name. I sat there, not knowing how to help.

"Her breathing is slowing!" shouted Ivory.

Some people started to scream. Even Blaire in the corner wasn't smirking anymore. Instead, she was rolling her eyes and grabbing her ear. I was about to go and punch her again, but that's how we got into this mess in the first place.

Mrs Serenity ran in. "What happened?"

"She passed out!" yelled Ivory as she pushed on Julianna's chest to get her to breathe properly.

By now everyone was screaming for Julianna to wake up (well, everyone except for Blaire), the whole cafeteria was almost crying, and Mrs Serenity was panicking.

"Come on Jules, you can't do this to me," said Ivory.

And then Julianna's chest rose with a shaky breath.

Chapter 6

Julianna: Still Standing

I jerked up abruptly. Everyone was staring at me. My breathing was fast and shallow. I wasn't sure if I was having a panic attack. Every part of me felt more sensitive. The bell rang and I winced at the noise.

"It's okay," said Ivory as she put her hand on mine.

"Everyone go to class," said Mrs Serenity, getting rid of the crowd.

"Here, drink some water," said Mateo, giving me the bottle.

"Thanks," I said as I slowly sipped the water while taking in breaths.

"I'm so sorry," said Addison.

"It's not your fault," I said.

'But why was she saying sorry?'

"What happened?" asked Avery.

"I don't know, I just felt weak," I said.

"Do you think you can get up?" asked Addison.

"I... I don't know," I said.

"It's okay, we'll help you," said Ivory.

Everyone (except Randy, who was playing with his Rubik's Cube) helped me get to the nurse's office.

"Just stay here for a while Jules," said Ivory.

I lay down on the bed, staring at the roof. Thoughts flooded my brain.

'Did everyone see what happened? Did they laugh? Who helped me?'

Suddenly Ms Patricia walked in.

'Oh great,' I thought.

She was always rude to me and never believed me when I passed out. She thought I was an attention seeker.

"Julianna, what did I say about faking?" snapped Ms Patricia, her voice sharp and cruel.

"Ms, I just passed out in the cafeteria."

Ms Patricia rolled her eyes. "Go back to class."

My stomach dropped. Shakily, I pushed myself upright, my vision blurring. Ivory shot forward before I could say another word.

"Excuse me?" Ivory's voice was sharper than I'd ever heard it. "She literally collapsed in front of the whole school, and you think she's faking?"

Ms Patricia's eyebrow twitched. "Watch your tone, young lady."

"No, you watch yours," Mateo cut in, "she hit the ground. She wasn't breathing right. You'd know if you'd been there instead of assuming she's lying."

I stared at the floor, heat burning my cheeks. Why did this always happen to me? But he didn't stop. His fists were clenched, jaw tight.

"She needs rest, not another one of your lectures."

Addison suddenly stepped forward. "She's right. I mean..." She stumbled, glancing at me like she wasn't sure she had the right. "I... I was there. She hit the ground hard. You can't just say she's faking it."

Ms Patricia's eyes narrowed, clearly not used to being challenged. For a second I thought she might actually send them all to detention. But instead, she sniffed and muttered, "Fine. Do what you want. But don't say I didn't warn you when she pulls this stunt again."

She stormed out, leaving the door to slam behind her.

I felt Ivory squeeze my shoulder gently. "Ignore her," she said, voice softer now. "She doesn't know what she's talking about." Mateo was still seething, but his eyes softened when he looked at me.

Chapter 7

Addison: The Start of Us

Once Julianna felt better we made our way to Geography. It was the worst because the teacher kept telling us stories about his life that no one cared about. I got bored and looked at the rest of the class. Julianna was reading under the desk, Ivory was balancing a pencil on her fingertips, Randy was solving a Rubik's Cube, Mateo flicked coins across the desk, grinning whenever one spun longer than the others. Avery put sunglasses on so that he could sleep and Blaire's minions looked like they were actually paying attention when she wasn't around.

As I was falling asleep, a screech of feedback exploded from the PA system. The sound ripped through the room like a gunshot. Ivory's pencil clattered to the floor. Randy dropped his cube with a curse. Mateo's last coin spun off the desk and hit Avery's shoe, jerking him awake. The whole class jolted upright as the speaker crackled to life.

"Addison Moore from year nine to the office... Addison Moore from year nine to the office please, thank you," said the PA.

I jumped up and realised I was a little bit too excited. I left my stuff in the classroom, thinking I would come back. I walked into the office happily and Mrs Serenity was sitting behind the table.

"Addison, go sit over there," said Mrs Serenity sweetly, but behind her smile I could tell something bad happened.

She pointed to the seat next to where Blaire was sitting. I rolled my eyes and sat down. Blaire was blotting her ear with a tissue. She was acting so dramatic, so I tried to stay as far away from her as I could, but it's kind of hard when you're sitting on a chair connected to another chair. Then a woman burst into the room.

"Addison Taylor Moore!" yelled a familiar voice.

It was my mum.

"Get in the car right now!" she yelled, even louder.

I didn't even have time to tell her that my stuff was still in the classroom before she gave me a one-hour lecture on the way home about how 'this isn't how I raised you' and 'apologise to that girl'

Once I got home, I threw myself onto my bed, got my boom box and blasted Madonna songs until my mum knocked on the door and told me to turn it off. I was so nervous about tomorrow and what everyone would think of me that I couldn't sleep.

The next day I wore simpler clothes to school: dark blue jeans, a black t-shirt and some white and black converse shoes. When I went downstairs, I saw my mum waiting in the kitchen with her arms crossed.

"Addison, you almost got suspended yesterday!" she shouted. "Go to school and don't get into any more fights!"

"Yes mum."

I walked out the door and headed for the bus stop.

After a long bus drive, I finally made it to school and saw Julianna at the gate with Mateo, Randy, Ivory and Avery. As soon as she saw me, she started jumping and waving at me while the rest were all trying to calm her down. I walked over to them.

"Hey guys, what's up?" I said enthusiastically.

"Girl, I kid you not, the whole school is talking about yesterday! It's only your second day of school and you're already a legend!" exclaimed Julianna.

"Jules, chill," said Mateo.

"Sorry, but Addi is amazing!"

A small voice came from behind me. "No, it was fantabulous!"

Ivory.

"It was wicked!" another voice said.

Avery.

"Oh, I almost forgot! Here's your stuff you left it yesterday," said Julianna, handing me my water bottle, pencil case and textbooks.

"Thanks," I said, smiling.

Suddenly the bell rang. "There goes the bell. Let's go to class," said Randy.

We walked to class, and I felt happy. Happier than I was at my other school, like I finally belonged, but that happiness would be gone in a matter of seconds, and I didn't even know it.

We were walking up the stairs and out of nowhere Blaire came the opposite way and shoved me. I fell down the stairs onto Julianna, and she fell onto Ivory, and we landed on the last step of the long staircase.

"Are you guys, okay?" asked Mateo.

"Does it look like we're okay?" snapped Ivory.

We helped each other up and kept walking to our next class, which was History. Once we were there, we had to get into our groups again, which I was happy with because all my friends were with me. The only person I wasn't friends with in that group was Blaire, and I didn't really know Blake. We started to plan our assignment. It was supposed to be about an activity people created in the 1940s, so we decided to pick roller-skating.

"There's an abandoned roller-skating warehouse near my house," said Mateo.

"Cool! We can go there for our assignment," said Julianna.

"Yeah, I'll give you guys the address. Does anyone have paper for me to write it on?"

"I do," said Ivory, passing him paper and a pen. He wrote down the address and gave it to everyone.

"Maybe we can make a poster about it!" said Randy excitedly.

We got to work, deciding what colours to use and of course doing research in the library using the encyclopedia. While Mateo, Julianna, Randy and I researched and wrote down points, Ivory and Avery started to make drafts of what the poster might look like. They were really good at drawing. Especially Avery.

Blake was still playing on his Game & Watch under his jacket and Blaire just looked at herself in her mini mirror, fixing her stupid permed hair.

"This is due in a month, right?" asked Avery.

"Yep," said Julianna.

"When do you think we should go to the factory?" asked Ivory.

"Probably in about one or two weeks," said Mateo.

"We should go in two weeks in case Mrs Lindsey adds any extra things," said Randy.

"Are you guys getting your parents to drive or do you need a ride?" asked Mateo.

"I need a ride," said Julianna.

"I think we all do. Our parents won't let us go to an abandoned warehouse on our own," said Ivory.

"I have a driver's licence, so I'll pick everyone up and drop everyone home," said Mateo.

"I'll give you my address," said Julianna.

"Me too," said Randy.

"Yeah, all of you guys give it to me," said Mateo.

"Wait, we're in Year 9, so how can you drive?" asked Randy.

"I have a fake ID."

Mrs Lindsey walked up to our group. "That doesn't sound like work over here."

Julianna looked up at her. "Mrs, we are planning where we should go and do research outside of school."

"Oh, I see." She walked off looking a little bit disappointed that she couldn't yell at us. Weird.

"So, Saturday in two weeks?" I asked.

"Yep," said Ivory.

"What are we doing?" asked Blaire.

"We are doing our project on roller-skates," said Julianna.

"What's a 'rolly' skate?"

Ivory looked pissed. "Blaire, you airhead."

"Shut up, you spaz."

"You wanna go?" said Ivory, closing her marker and standing up facing Blaire. She was a lot shorter than Blaire but still looked intimidating.

"Bite me!" spat Blaire.

I rolled my eyes. She still can't even come up with new comebacks.

Ivory rolled up her sleeves. "Alright you bimbette."

"Ooh!" we all said in unison.

Blaire rolled her eyes. "You are so lame."

"Better to be lame than to be a ditz like you."

"Bitchin'" someone whispered.

Blaire smirked and crossed her arms. "If awkward had a mascot, it would be you."

Something changed in Ivory's eyes, like she was about to drag Blaire's whole life.

"Wow, all that hair and none of the brains? Impressive commitment to style over substance."

Julianna's eyes lit up as she whispered, "Total burn."

"Bag your face," said Blaire.

"No, I won't, you mall-maggot."

"Damn," someone whispered.

"Wow, your personality really screams background decoration," said Blaire.

"If being obnoxious were a sport, you'd have more gold than Marita Koch."

"Did she just...?" asked someone with admiration.

"You're a barf bag!" Blaire yelled.

"Alright you space cadet!"

"Ooh!" we all said in unison.

"Girls, what is going on here?" yelled Mrs Lindsey.

"Mrs, Blaire was being rude to Ivory," blurted Randy, who wasn't even watching the drama.

He was just playing with his Rubik's Cube.

Ivory did her innocent face at the exact moment he said that.

"Blaire! Lunch detention!" yelled Mrs Lindsey. She walked away.

Blaire rolled her eyes. "Ugh, this is bogus. I didn't even do anything wrong. You called me an airhead first!"

"Maybe if you helped with the project I wouldn't have called you that!" Ivory yelled back.

"Blake, I didn't do anything wrong, did I?" asked Blaire innocently as she batted her giant, fake eyelashes.

"Shut up, bimbo," said Blake, still distracted by his Game & Watch.

As soon as the bell rang Blaire stormed off dramatically, while the rest of us walked together to each other's lockers.

Julianna enveloped her in a hug. "Ive, that was radical!"

"Yeah, Ive that was wicked!" exclaimed Avery.

"Thanks, I've hated Blaire my whole life, but I was too scared to stand up to her until Addi stood up to her yesterday."

She smiled at me, and I smiled back. That's when I realised that everyone was actually scared of Blaire and that's why most people leave her alone.

I wanted to change that.

At recess Julianna had to go to the library, Mateo had soccer practice, Randy had to go to the computer lab and Avery had to go to band practice, so me and Ivory hung out.

"I like your necklace," I said.

"Thanks," she replied, "I love gardening, so I always wear flower accessories."

"What plants do you have?"

"I have some lilies, an ivy plant and daisies, and I planted that big tree over there," said Ivory pointing to a giant oak tree.

"Wow!"

"And whenever new people move in, I plant a rose bush in front of their house. It's like my welcome gift."

"Wait, that was you?"

"Yeah, I did for most people here."

"That's so kind of you."

She smiled.

The bell rang and we all went to our next classes, and I had the best day ever. Me and my friends hung out the whole day, making jokes and having fun like there was nothing to worry about. We all sat together at the cafeteria and that's when I saw Blaire, with the fakest tears I had ever seen, leading principal Davis right toward our table.

"All of you, after school detention for one hour," said Principal Davis.

"Why?" asked Mateo.

"Because you guys are bullying Blaire," said principal Davis, pointing at Blaire while she wiped invisible tears.

"No one is bullying Blaire," said Julianna, confused.

"You guys always bully me," said Blaire, now fake crying.

"Principal, do you really believe someone like Blaire?" asked Ivory.

"After school detention for two hours Miss Pearce," said Principal Davis.

"If you give my sister extra detention then you give me extra detention," said Avery.

"Fine, two-hour detention for you as well."

"If you give them detention, you give me detention too," said Mateo.

"You also get extra detention."

"I'll take extra detention if they get it!" said Julianna.

"You've got it!"

"Me too!" I said happily.

"Okay."

"Aww what the heck. Me too!" said Randy.

"Fine, you all have two hours detention after school."

"What an idiot," whispered Mateo.

"I heard that, Ramirez" said Principal Davis.

Mateo gulped.

"Three hours of detention."

"Yeah, I'm not staying that long," said Randy.

"You're on your own, man," said Avery.

"Damn," said Mateo.

We had our boring English class and Art class and when they were over it was three-twenty, which meant detention time. While everyone, including Blaire, got to talk and hang out after school, my friends and I had to go to the dark, cramped detention room. The blinds were closed and there were no lights. Everyone there all looked like they were depressed and hadn't slept in days. Some were doing homework and others were doodling in sketchbooks. A girl was drawing a black heart in the corner of her Science homework and a boy was drawing skulls all over his Maths book cover. We shuffled towards the back, trying not to draw attention.

I slid into the seat between Ivory and Julianna. Avery and Randy dropped into the row behind us, Randy immediately pulling out, you guessed it, his Rubik's Cube, while Avery leaned back like he was about to nap through the apocalypse. Mateo sat in front of us, drumming his fingers on the desk restlessly, and Julianna was reading her book.

The teacher in charge was Mr Hayes, who looked like he'd rather be *anywhere* else. He sat at the front reading a mystery novel, not even looking up when we came in. The only time he made a sound was when someone whispered too loudly. Then he barked, "Quiet!" before going right back to his book.

We exchanged knowing looks. If the grown-ups weren't going to pay attention, we'd make our own fun. So, my friends and I passed notes. Ivory was the first. Her note read, *I'm sorry you guys have to stay here an extra hour because of me.*

Before I could reply, Julianna grabbed the note and scribbled across the bottom in big bubble letters:

Don't be silly, detention with friends is better than detention alone!

She even drew a little cartoon of us behind bars with goofy grins. Ivory laughed quietly, and even Mateo cracked a smirk. We all smiled at her and wrote things like

All good, not your fault and *Blaire deserved it.*

When notes got boring, we switched to hand gestures, half sign language, half nonsense. Mateo whispered, pretending to translate like some TV host, Julianna, Ivory and I did anything to not burst out laughing. From behind us came the steady *click-click* of Randy's cube. If I heard that noise in my sleep, I wouldn't be surprised. Avery didn't even glance up, just shaded the corner of a drawing in his sketchbook with an almost destroyed pencil, his tongue poking out slightly between his lips in concentration. Ivory leaned back on her chair, whispering without moving her lips, "I'll trade you my pencil if you write me a better comeback for Blaire."

After about thirty minutes I fell asleep. Then I felt someone tapping me. It was Ivory. I lifted my head and turned to her.

"Detention's over," she said, pulling me up.

"See you guys tomorrow," whispered Mateo.

But then Julianna froze, staring at her desk with a mischievous grin. Before anyone could stop her, she stood, grabbed the desk, and lifted it off the floor.

"Jules!" Ivory hissed.

She threw it at the front of the classroom and the desk clattered to the ground with a bang.

"Ow my arm," said Julianna as she rubbed her arm.

"One hour extra detention," said Mr Hayes.

"Okay," said Julianna, smiling as she grabbed another desk and sat down.

We waved bye to her and Mateo.

Julianna waved cheerfully back, like she hadn't just sentenced herself to another hour in hell. Mateo stared at her, shocked about the fact that she threw a desk.

"I need to call my mum to pick me up," said Randy.

"Same," I said.

"Ivory, I'll call Mum to pick us up," said Avery.

Everyone's mums said that they would pick them up. Except mine.

My mum screamed at me for getting detention on the second day of school and then told me that I had to catch the last bus home. I waited for the six forty-five bus, waving goodbye to my friends as I watched them get picked up by their parents. I wished my mum would do that for me. I understood why she was mad, but I was still upset. The sun went down and I didn't have a jacket, so I sat at the bus stop, freezing. That's when Mateo and Julianna walked up to me. Julianna looked concerned.

"Hey, why are you still here?"

"My mum wouldn't pick me up," I said.

"You should have thrown a desk like Jules and stayed with us," Mateo teased.

We all started laughing.

"Honestly thought that was insane!" he said.

We kept laughing. No one would believe us if we said that Jules threw a desk, but I guess I saw a new side of her today.

Suddenly the bus pulled up, and we all got on. It was full because people were getting back from work. I had to stand up, while Mateo sat next to some people he knew and Julianna sat in an empty seat which she offered to me first, but I told her to take it.

Once I got home my mum was waiting at the door with her arms crossed.

"Addison, what has gotten into you!" yelled my mum.

"Nothing," I said.

"Why are you being a bully?"

"I'm not a bully. I'm being bullied."

I stormed up the stairs into my room and didn't come down for dinner even though I was starving. I just wanted to be alone. I wished Blaire would leave me alone or move to a different school, but we all know neither of those is going to happen.

The next day I got up, put on a grey hoodie and jeans and left for school before my mum woke up. I caught the six-thirty bus. On the bus I did some homework and that's when Ivory and Avery got on the bus. Ivory plopped down in the seat next to me.

"Hopefully Blaire doesn't try to get us in trouble again."

"Yeah, hopefully."

When we got to school there was barely anyone there. It looked abandoned and felt creepy, especially near my locker. It was foggy. Too foggy. It was hard to see anything. I got everything I needed for my next lessons, which were History and Geography. Then suddenly someone pulled my hair so hard that I fell backwards.

I turned around to find Blaire and her minions laughing like witches behind me. They were worse than witches.

"She's so stupid!" said one of Blaire's minions, dying of laughter.

"Yeah, like totally!" laughed one of Blaire's other minions.

"Hey, shoo, get out of here!" yelled a familiar voice. It was Julianna. She appeared at the end of the hall like some kind of avenging angel; her books clutched to her chest. Her expression wasn't sweet this time. It was sharp, protective. Blaire and her minions ran off giggling. I quickly got up and saw all my friends.

"Are you okay?" asked Ivory.

"Yeah, I'm fine," I said, annoyed.

"Ignore them, they're just stupid little bi…" said Julianna who was cut off by Mrs Lindsey.

"Language, Miss Kim."

After Mrs Lindsey left, Julianna rolled her eyes as she whispered "*jeongmal nappeun nyeon-iya.*"

"The bell's gonna ring in five minutes," said Randy.

"Let's go," said Avery.

We headed to the Geography room and tried to sit close to each other. Ivory, Julianna and I sat together, and Mateo, Randy and Avery sat behind us.

The Geography teacher started his boring stories again.

"Back when I was your age," he began, sitting on his desk, mug in hand, "I spent the summer working at a map shop in Denver. You wouldn't believe how complicated people found coordinates."

I zoned out straightaway. My friends and I passed notes and tried not to laugh at Ivory's caricatures of Blaire. One of them was Blaire with devil horns. I almost choked on my water. Julianna bit down on her cheek to stifle a laugh and I caught Avery smirking behind us. Ivory burned the evidence when she asked to go to the bathroom so that we didn't get in trouble for 'bullying' again. I heard people whispering about how there were people who mutated because of radiation, which was really weird.

At recess Ivory had to go to the school gardens, so me and Julianna were hanging out.

"What's your favourite hobby?" I asked.

"Surfing, definitely!" exclaimed Julianna.

"Is that why you have an ocean bracelet?"

"Kind of," said Julianna, lifting up her wrist to show the bracelet. "My whole family knows that I'm obsessed with the ocean, so my grandmother made me this bracelet."

"That's so nice!"

"Thanks!"

That's when the bell rang and we had to go to our next lesson which was History. We got into our groups again and continued working on the project.

"Guys, I just realised that I can't do Saturday in two weeks, but I can do this Saturday," said Mateo.

"Oh my gosh, same. I was going to sneak out of my window because people were coming over," said Julianna, laughing.

"So, this Saturday?" asked Randy.

"Yep," I said.

"Random question," said Julianna. "What is everyone's favourite colour?"

"Green," said Ivory. "It reminds me of plants.

"Orange," said Randy, "because it's the first side of my Rubik's Cube that finishes."

"Purple," said Avery. "It makes me feel focused."

"I like green too," I said, "It reminds me of my old bedroom, which had green walls."

"My favourite is red," said Mateo. "It reminds me of fire, and I really like fire."

"What's your favourite, Jules?" asked Ivory.

"Blue," said Julianna, "because it reminds me of the ocean."

Each colour they chose represented them so perfectly.

The rest of the day was pretty boring. We did normal work in English and Art. Blaire didn't annoy us, or even talk to us, and I didn't get in trouble. I got home and my mum actually didn't yell at me, not even about what happened yesterday. I listened to music and came down for dinner, and I finally slept peacefully.

At least that's what I wish happened.

Chapter 8

Addison: Total Chaos

What really happened was after History, at the cafeteria. As usual, the smell of oily pizza plagued the room. I was walking with my food (spaghetti and meatballs and it wasn't oily) when one of Blaire's minions tripped me. I fell, with my spaghetti and meatballs, onto Blaire, who was wearing her white designer top.

She looked like she was about to pass out.

Everyone in the cafeteria was shocked, including me.

"You airhead!" she yelled at the top of her lungs.

"Sorry. I guess," I said.

It was her minion's fault anyway.

Then, as I was walking away, Blaire picked up a meatball and hurled it at me. It hit me right in the back of my head. I fell forward, barely catching myself on a table.

"Alright that's it!" yelled Julianna, slamming her tray on the table. "FOOD FIGHT!"

The whole cafeteria was throwing food at each other and screaming. Blaire was going insane; all the meatball sauce splashed on her designer shirt and in her hair. I could see Ivory using her tray as a shield, Mateo throwing spring rolls and ducking under the table, as if they were grenades. Randy sat under the table playing with his Rubik's Cube. Avery was trying to save his sketchbook from all the food and Julianna — actually I couldn't see Julianna anywhere. Then suddenly she ran at me.

"Get down!" she cried as she tackled me to the ground.

I looked up to see Blaire's bright neon-pink lunch tray fly right over our heads.

"Thanks Jules," I said, relieved.

"No problem."

Suddenly Principal Davis stormed into the cafeteria. Everyone froze. I could swear even the meatball stopped moving in midair.

"Who did this!?" shouted Principal Davis.

"Blaire did!" yelled Randy, not looking up from his Rubik's Cube.

"Blaire, three hours' detention after school!"

Blaire started fake, ugly crying. Her mascara dripped from her lashes like shadows dissolving in water.

"Sir if you check the security footage, you'll see that Addison actually spilled meatball sauce on me first! Julianna screamed 'food fight' and Randy is lying!"

"Let us check the footage shall we, Miss Pembroke?"

I gulped as we walked to Principal Davis's office. He turned the TV on and my stomach dropped.

Me, Blaire's minion who tripped me, Julianna and Randy all had three hours of detention again.

"CRASH!"

We all turned around to find Mateo standing near a broken desk.

"Ramirez, did you do this?" screamed Principal Davis.

"Yeah, now give me detention," said Mateo.

"Three hours' detention," said Principal Davis.

We all went to our next class, which was English. We had to work on some Shakespeare stuff (I wasn't really paying attention).

"Hey, where's Ivory?" asked Julianna.

"She's in the sick bay," said Avery.

"What happened?" I asked.

"Someone threw spaghetti sauce in her eye," said Avery. "I threw my tray at them after, and they slammed into a wall."

We all gawked at him.

"Slammed into a wall?" asked Mateo.

Avery nodded like it was normal.

When the bell rang Ivory and Avery went home and the rest of us went to Art.

"Today we will be painting," said Mrs Mia, the art teacher.

She handed out the paint, and we started on our landscapes. Suddenly Blaire threw her paint at my hair, turning it a sticky bright pink and green.

"Blaire! Detention after school for three hours," said Mrs Mia.

"Whatever," said Blaire.

Julianna tried to help me get the paint out of my hair, but some of it wouldn't come out. The lesson ended and we went to detention. It was boring this time because we had a really strict teacher who kept walking around checking if we were talking or passing notes. After that long detention I caught the 6:45 bus home. Once again, my mum was angry, but I just zoned out when she yelled at me.

Thursday was a blur of pop quizzes and homework.

But then came the day no one expected.

It was Friday morning. Ivory, Avery, Randy, Mateo, Julianna and I were sitting in class, talking about going to the warehouse the next day. Suddenly Blaire came up to us.

"Hey losers."

I rolled my eyes and sighed, "What do you want, Blaire?"

"I'm having a party today, and I felt bad not inviting you."

"What?" asked Ivory.

"Yeah, the whole school's invited," said Blaire "Here's the address and time."

Blaire walked back to her minions, but she didn't laugh or point at us. Which was surprising.

"Should we go?" I asked, "It might be fun."

"Sure," said Avery, not looking up from his sketchbook.

"I don't see why not," said Randy.

"Yeah, I'll come," said Ivory.

"Umm, okay I'll come" said Julianna, sounding almost hesitant and not as bubbly as she usually was.

"If you guys all come, I'll come," said Mateo.

The rest of the day basically flew past. With a Maths pop quiz and some Science homework. We were soon outside and about to go home.

"Okay, so we'll carpool," said Ivory.

"Yeah, I'll pick you guys up," said Mateo.

We all left to go home. I walked because the bus was full. Home was only a fifteen-minute walk, and it was safe because school had just ended.

Luckily, Mum works overtime on Fridays so she wouldn't suspect a thing. I rummaged through my closet and didn't find anything good to wear.

"Why don't I have any good clothes?" I muttered to myself.

Then an idea clicked in my brain. My mum and I are the same size in shoes and clothes.

Jackpot!

I went to her room and looked through her closet. I found the most perfect outfit: a black mini stretch dress and some black stiletto heels.

'*Perfect*,' I thought.

I put the outfit on and straightened my hair. After that was done I did my make-up, subtle but still noticeable. I looked out the window to see a black convertible waiting outside. All my friends were in it. "Addi, come on!" yelled Julianna.

"Shut up," said the neighbour, Mr Smith. He was old and had sensitive hearing.

"Sorry," whispered Julianna, but loud enough for him to hear.

"Coming!" I called out.

I ran to the car, wobbling in my heels. I opened the door and saw everyone was already in there. Julianna wore a blue mini stretch dress, blue flats and of course her famous bracelet, while Ivory wore her flower necklace, green mini stretch dress, an oversized sherpa-lined denim jacket and black and white Converse.

'Bold choice,' I thought to myself.

I was impressed.

"You guys look like you're going to prom and a concert at the same time," said Avery, while sketching.

"Prom, concert, whatever," I said, "Blaire's not going to know what hit her when we show up like this."

"Let's go!" said Julianna.

In the car we blasted all kinds of music: Prince, Madonna, Michael Jackson, Cyndi Lauper and even Bruce Springsteen.

By the time we got there the party was already in full swing. You could hear it from down the street. From the window you could see that there were way too many people in one tiny house.

"Let's stick together," said Ivory, nervously tugging at her necklace.

"Right," Randy said, already eyeing the snack table through the front window. "Together."

Strobe lights borrowed from someone's older sibling blinded everyone. The DJ, in this case a short, thirteen-year-old boy with a goofy grin named Troy with a boom box and a tangle of cassette tapes swapped a tape and blasted 'Footloose'. The entire living room looked like a music video. And then I saw Blaire. She sat on the arm of the couch like she owned the place, laughing at something a boy said, one hand tossing her giant tragedy of hair.

The second we walked into the living room the music froze for just a moment, enough that heads turned our way. Kids in denim jackets and oversized sweaters froze, staring. Our dresses practically glowed under the strobe lights.

Blaire looked us up and down. "Well, well, well," she said, loud enough for the whole room to hear. "Looks like prom night came early. What's the theme? Trying too hard?"

Her minions laughed on cue, though a few kids in the crowd looked more impressed than amused.

"She's jealous," I whispered to Julianna and Ivory.

Ivory smirked and folded her arms. "Or threatened."

Blaire tossed her curls back, pretending not to care. But the way her grin faltered told us everything: she hated that we'd stolen the spotlight.

Troy blasted Prince's 'Let's Go Crazy'. Teens whooped and started dancing. Someone bumped my shoulder, then said, "Sorry!" without looking back. We drifted toward the snacks because that's what you do when you don't know where else to stand. Randy grabbed a plate and started stacking chips like he was about to go into hibernation.

"Dude," said Mateo, "save some for the economy."

Randy shrugged, cheeks puffed with chips. "It's called bulking, but let's just hope there's no nuts."

We all laughed. I grabbed a can of soda and cracked it open. Avery had one too.

"Guys, how about a chugging contest," said Mateo.

"I'm down," said Avery.

"Sure," I said.

Soon enough someone saw us and yelled, "Avery and the new girl are having a chugging contest!"

Everyone stared at us and started chanting, "Addison! Avery! Addison! Avery!"

My nose started to burn, and I could tell Avery was also struggling. Suddenly I felt like I couldn't swallow. I started choking and Avery did too because he got startled. We both began coughing. Julianna patted my back, trying to stop my coughing. Ivory slammed Avery's back to help him, though I'm not sure if it really helped. People started booing, but after a minute they went back to dancing.

"Are you guys, okay?" asked Mateo.

"I'm fine," I said, wheezing.

"Same," Avery mumbled.

"Ivory, isn't that your fourth can of soda?" asked Julianna.

"Fifth," she hiccupped. We all started laughing.

"Why?" I asked still laughing

"For nerves," she said. Then she hiccupped again.

After about half an hour someone tugged my arm. "Addi!"

I turned around and it was Ivory, her eyes wild.

"What's up?" I asked.

"Dance with me."

She dragged me to the dance floor, where 'PYT (Pretty Young Thing)' was playing. I didn't do anything too flashy, just a couple of twirls and shooting arms up, but she was bouncing and looked like she was going to explode if she stopped moving. Suddenly Blaire stood up on the table and started shouting, "Truth or dare."

Soon enough everyone was chanting.

"Addison! Truth or dare?" asked some random kid from our class.

"Dare," I said.

Some people were disappointed, while others looked hyped up. Blaire pushed past the person who asked me, "I dare you to dance solo in the centre of the room."

I wasn't about to chicken out against Blaire, so I stepped forward in those high heels and looked over at Troy. He looked like he knew a perfect song but just couldn't find it. He finally grabbed a cassette and grinned. He put on 'Girls Just Want To Have Fun', my favourite Cyndi Lauper song. I whipped out the best dance moves ever. People were cheering. I caught Blaire rolling her eyes. I smirked and then started breakdancing. There were 'oohs' and 'ahhs' everywhere. This was the first time I had fun at a party in a long time. I bowed fancily at the end, and the party erupted in claps and cheers, but Blaire wasn't about to let the spotlight slip away. She smirked and snapped her fingers.

"Dance battle. Us versus you. Right now."

"Bet," said Ivory as she took off her jacket and tossed it at Avery.

Troy's eyes lit up like he had been waiting for this moment all his life. He reached into his box of cassettes and held up a tape like it was pure gold.

"Got this one straight from my cousin in Miami. Not even out here yet. It's called 'Conga!'"

He slammed it into the boom box.

Blaire and her crew stepped up first. They stomped to the beat, snapping their fingers and tossing their curls in sync. Their moves were dramatic, all hips and hair, but stiff, like a commercial trying too hard. The crowd clapped along, but they didn't look like they were enjoying it.

Then it was our turn. We locked eyes and suddenly I knew what moves to do, like we had practiced it a million times. We stepped forward in a clean line. On the first downbeat, we slammed our shoes to the floor, snapping into a sharp side-step in sync. Hands shot up. Spin. Clap. Drop low. Each move snapped like it had been rehearsed for months, but it was pure chemistry, just three friends moving as if they shared one brain.

The crowd screamed.

"They are killing it!" yelled someone.

"Oh my god, they're like a girl group!" someone exclaimed.

Blaire's group went again.

Clarissa lunged into a spin too early and tripped over a lamp cord making the lamp fall on the table where a half-filled soda can sat. There was a mess of soda on the carpet and table, and a couple of people yelped because of the splash. She fell flat on her back. A boy tried to drag her out of the circle, but she shoved back in, her cheeks flaming.

Then came the chorus.

I clapped overhead, Julianna and Ivory instantly falling in on either side. All three of us twisted our hips to the rhythm, arms circling fluidly before breaking apart and snapping back together with a sharp freeze pose. Then Ivory and I looked at each other and nodded like we knew exactly what to do. We stood next to each other and Julianna sprinted and jumped, landing on our palms before we pushed her off and she flipped — not one but two flips midair — and landed perfectly. I felt unstoppable. The crowd erupted like it was the best performance in the world and they had front row seats.

Larissa tried to dip Geniessa dramatically, similar to how we had flipped Julianna, but her grip slipped. Geniessa yelped as she dropped flat on her butt, the crowd roaring with laughter. She scrambled up, cheeks red. Determined, she launched into a cartwheel. But her foot hit the lamp that Clarissa had already knocked over, sending it crashing into the wall. Gasps shot through the crowd, then laughter bubbled up. Blaire's fake smile faltered into a scowl, but she pretended not to notice, still stomping and pointing to the ceiling, sweat glistening at her temples.

The minions tried to recover with way too many hair tosses, but they weren't in sync. One flipped left, another flipped right, and the third nearly smacked Blaire in the face with her curls. The crowd's laughter drowned out the music for a second.

That's when Julianna, Ivory and I stepped up, smooth, sharp and perfectly in sync. The contrast was brutal. We finished with a flourish, me hitting the splits dead centre, Julianna spinning into a clean hair flip, Ivory leaning back into a perfect freeze pose with arms crossed. The three of us turned together, slow, deliberate, then focused our eyes on Blaire. All three of us smirked as the room exploded.

"Add-i-son! Jul-i-an-na! Iv-o-ry!"

But Ravenwood had a thing about good things not lasting long.

"Addison!" yelled Blaire "Truth or dare!".

"But she just…" started Clarissa.

"Shh," Blaire hissed.

That's when I made a big mistake.

"Truth."

"Why did you move to Ravenwood?" asked Blaire.

My stomach dropped.

"We needed a change of pace," I said quickly.

"Is that what you like to tell yourself?" asked Blaire.

"It's the truth," I said.

Then Blaire decided to strike again, but her target wasn't me this time.

Chapter 9

Ivory: Crossing the Line

I was electric, way more than usual. My moves were all sharp, my footwork fast, almost *too* fast. Every spin came with a little stumble, and I turned it into style. I hiccupped as I clapped and people cheered, thinking it was part of the routine.

"Dude, she's unstoppable!" someone yelled.

What they didn't know? I had downed at least twelve cans of soda. I was buzzing, eyes wild, hands shaking between moves. Still, when we hit the finisher, Addison's splits, Julianna's flawless hair spin, my freeze with arms crossed, the crowd went wild, chanting our names. I couldn't stop bouncing.

Then Blaire asked Addison why she moved to Ravenwood and called her out for lying. Then she chose a new target.

Me.

Blaire grinned like a manic. "Blake," She called out sweetly "It's time."

Blake walked over, smirking, for once not with his Game & Watch. He had something else. Something familiar. He gave it to Blaire, and she held it up with a huge smile like it was the best thing in the world.

A Walkman with the name *Ivory Pearce* written on it. My stomach dropped.

"Shit," I whispered under my breath, heart racing.

"Let's see what our shy little Ivory listens to," said Blaire, grinning like a devil.

"No…" I started, but Blaire hit the play button.

Wake Me Up Before You Go-Go! blasted out. Everyone started laughing and I just wanted to disappear into the ground. Until Avery gave me a note.

Here's that comeback you wanted :)

I smirked and looked at Blaire. "I like it. At least it's better than your personality."

The room filled with cheers, gasps, and horrified looks.

"Say that again," said Blaire, stepping forward.

I stepped closer. "I like it. It's better than your personality," I said, enunciating each word clearly.

Blaire smirked. "Oh, look at that, the plant girl finally grows a spine."

Then she turned and loudly said to the crowd, "Guess even background characters get dialogue sometimes."

My jaw clenched and I took another step forward. When someone grabbed my wrist.

I turned.

Julianna.

"Ive, don't do it" she whispered.

I shook her arm off and grabbed the nearest cup of soda. I threw it right at Blaire's face. Soda, dripping down her designer shirt and fake curls. Blaire's whole face went red, and she lunged to shove me. That's when Avery and Addison got in between us, fists ready. As if they rehearsed this.

"Back off," said Addison.

The air shifted. Tense and sharp. Everyone was waiting for a fight, and I don't think they were going to leave without one.

Chapter 10

Addison: Everything at Once

Blaire shoved me first. Hard. The lamp behind me fell and smashed. A piece of glass shot into my calf. I cried out and wobbled forward. Avery shoved Blaire back, harder. A boy from Blaire's swarm lunged at him. Mateo came forward and swung, his fist connecting with the boy's temple. The room erupted in chaos. Everyone was screaming, sodas spilled everywhere, porcelain pieces smashed to the ground. I dove onto Blaire despite the throbbing pain in my leg.

Then Randy coughed. At first it sounded like he'd swallowed wrong, but then he collapsed. His lips swelled, his face was blotchy, and his eyes went wide.

"Allergic reaction!" someone screamed.

Panic filled the house. Half the party was fighting while the other half watched Randy. Suddenly from the corner of my eye I saw it. Julianna ran to get a water bottle. She already looked pale, but when she came back half of our group was fighting and bleeding. Her knee buckled. She collapsed. No one caught her in time.

"Julianna!" I shrieked, tearing myself from Blaire. Mateo ripped away from the boys clawing at him and dropped beside her.

Avery pressed two fingers to her throat. "She's breathing," he said, voice tight.

"Randy isn't!" yelled Ivory.

He was still wheezing. My hands dove into his jacket, nothing. Then his jeans pocket. I yanked the EpiPen free and jammed it into his thigh. Click. One, two, three, his chest jerked and breath rattled back into him.

"We need to get them to the hospital," I shouted.

Suddenly Ivory hiccupped so hard her back smacked the wall.

"I... I don't feel so good," she whispered, her words slurring. Her eyes were wide and unfocused, hands trembling.

Avery caught her just before she collapsed. "She's burning out. Too much soda, she's crashing."

For a second I thought she was going to throw up right there, but instead her knees buckled and she sagged in Avery's arms, pale and shaking.

"Ivory, stay with me," he barked, slapping her cheek lightly. Her head lolled and a hiccup rattled out of her chest.

"Not Ivory too," I muttered, panic choking me. Three of us were down. It felt impossible.

The front door slammed.

Parents.

"Everybody out!" they shouted.

Panic detonated. Kids bolted for doors, windows, yelling about cops. A boy vaulted over the couch like he had done this a million times; a girl knocked over a plant as she ran; someone slipped and fell hard on the fallen soil.

Avery and Mateo hauled Julianna up between them, Ivory hanging like deadweight on Avery's other arm. I hooked both hands under Randy's shoulders and dragged. We shoved a path through the kitchen, tore open the sliding door, and burst into the backyard. The parents were still chasing us. We ran until there was a fence with no gate.

"Shit!" spat Mateo.

The parents were closing in fast.

"Avery, give me a boost," slurred Ivory, barely coherent but stubborn.

Avery let go of Julianna and dropped to one knee. Ivory scrambled onto his back, nearly slipping as her sneaker slid off his shoulder. Avery grunted, shoving upward, and Ivory hauled herself over the top of the fence. She slammed down on the other side with a painful thud.

"Quick!" she yelled as she pushed herself up, palms bleeding. "Get Julianna on this side!"

Mateo and Avery locked arms under Julianna and heaved. She was limp, her head lolling. For a heart-stopping second, her foot caught on the fence. I thought she'd crash, but Ivory grabbed her wrists and dragged her safely down.

Next, we got Randy over and Ivory didn't even try to catch him. He was way too heavy for her.

Avery jumped over and so did Mateo. I was about to climb over when one of the parents grabbed me by the leg. I cried out as they dragged me on the grass, their nails digging into my ankles.

"Addi!" yelled Ivory. She wasn't thinking straight and tried to jump over the fence to get me. Avery pulled her back. The parent kept dragging me towards the house, grass and dirt flying on my face. Suddenly a figure appeared: it was Troy the DJ. He fly-kicked the parent in the chest. The parent lost their grip on my leg.

"Go!" Troy barked.

My shoe fell off, but there was no time for that. I wiped my face with my forearm, jumped over the fence and yelled out, "Thanks!"

We ran. Which wasn't easy. Me wearing one heel with glass still stuck in the back of my leg dragging Randy as he stumbled on the road, Mateo and Avery carrying Julianna and dragging Ivory's arm at the same time.

I wobbled to the nearest payphone and rummaged through my pocket for a coin.

"Here, I have one," slurred Ivory, putting the coin into my palm.

I dialled the emergency service.

"Hi, we have a girl passed out but breathing, another girl is having a bad sugar crash and a boy, he just had an allergic reaction to nuts," I said, panicked.

What the voice said back haunted me. "Listen, we get calls like this every Friday and Saturday, what is wrong with you people?"

"No, we actually..."

Click.

She hung up.

I gawked at the phone, and I could feel tears streaming down my face. They weren't coming.

"Are they coming?" slurred Ivory.

"She hung up," I whispered.

"What?" barked Mateo.

"She thought I was faking," I said.

"What the hell!?" said Avery as he punched the payphone so hard that the metal bent.

We were six helpless and stupid teens with cuts and bruises, wearing party clothes, and we had no idea what to do. I sat down on the pavement, looking around at everyone. Mateo and Avery put Julianna down on top of a jacket. They both had busted noses and lips. Ivory looked exhausted and had cut her leg when she fell onto the other side of the fence. She sat on the pavement,

"Don't... let me... fall asleep," she whispered, eyes fluttering. "If I sleep... I won't wake up."

Avery looked at her, exhausted. "Don't say that."

Randy's eyes started to droop. I tried to breathe. I hadn't realised that I had been holding one long breath the entire time. I leaned my head onto the cold payphone, wishing we hadn't come to the stupid party in the first place. It was my fault. I told them to come. Julianna hadn't looked like she even wanted to. Maybe she only came because the rest of us did.

I silently cried tears of regret.

Then Julianna jerked her head up.

Chapter 11

Julianna: Through the Haze

I snapped myself awake. I had so many questions. Everything was spinning. My ears were ringing like the music was still blasting, but the only sound now was our ragged breathing. I looked around. We were all out on the street. I was sitting on someone's jacket, Ivory looked like she was going to pass out, Mateo and Avery looked like they had just been in a boxing match, Addison was crying by a payphone and Randy's whole face was swollen.

Ivory turned around and saw me. "Jules!" she yelled as she stumbled to me. She hugged me tight like if she let go the world would end. She looked really pale and I noticed her clutching onto her necklace with one hand.

"What happened?" I asked.

"Parents came and chased us," said Mateo, looking back to make sure no one was following us.

I looked over at Addison. Tears were rolling down her cheeks.

"Addison, it's okay," said Avery.

"Yeah, Julianna is okay," said Ivory.

Addison spun her head around and hugged me.

"Oh Jules," she whispered.

"Do you think you can walk?" asked Ivory.

"I think so," I said.

Ivory helped me up and when she let go of my hands, my knees buckled and I went straight down again. They all grabbed my arm just before I hit the ground (everyone except Randy).

"Yeah, you're not walking," said Addison.

"Come on, we need to go back home before we get in trouble," said Randy.

"Are you going to be okay?" asked Addison.

"Yeah," he said.

We wobbled down the dimly lit street like a broken army, everyone leaning on everyone else. Mateo and Avery supported me between them, each limping with their own cuts and bruises. Ivory stumbled beside us, still clutching her necklace, clenching her jaw like she was forcing herself not to pass out for the sake of all of us. Addison stayed near Randy, her hand steadying him every few steps.

The car was parked a block away. The silence was louder than any music Troy had blasted at the party. Streetlights shone across our exhausted faces, and every adult voice in the distance made us flinch. One by one we were dropped off at our houses, slipping back into the night as if we hadn't just survived chaos.

Chapter 12

Ivory: Caught in the Quiet

Avery and I were dropped home first. He tried to help me out, but I told him I was fine, clutching my necklace like it gave me strength. I wobbled up the front steps, nearly tripping. For a second, I thought I'd collapse, but I turned back, forcing a weak smile at Julianna before sneaking inside. The porch light flickered off behind me. Our parents were waiting for us by the stairs, arms crossed, looking like they were going to kill.

"Where were you two?" demanded my mum, hands on her hips and her voice sharp and low.

"School project," I said, wrapping my jacket tighter so she wouldn't see my green dress underneath.

"Then why do you have a cut?" snapped my dad.

"I... I fell down the library steps," I said.

"Go to bed!" my dad barked, making both me and Avery flinch. We quickly went upstairs to our rooms. I peeled off the green dress and shoved it under my bed. Then I put my pyjamas on and wrapped a bandage around my giant cut. I collapsed on my bed.

The thoughts flooded through my mind.

I lay back and stared at the ivy on my bedside table. I named it Saphy when I was six years old. It was my friend. Back in primary school when Blaire still bullied me for being 'the plant girl.' I drowned in my thoughts until suddenly the phone rang.

Chapter 13

Julianna: The Lines we Cross

I was the last one to get dropped home. I quietly opened the door and there they were. My parents. They were standing at the bottom of the stairs, looking like they had been waiting there for hours.

"Where were you, Julianna?" asked my mum, her hands on her hips. She looked furious.

"I was doing a school project at the library," I responded.

My dad's eyes narrowed. "Wearing that?"

I looked down at my outfit. A blue mini stretch dress. Definitely not something you would wear to the library.

"You're grounded!" snapped my dad.

Behind them, my older brother and sister stood near the stairs. Their faces were stiff with disapproval. Neither said a word. They didn't need to. The silence was enough. I went up to my room and sat on my bed. I didn't even bother getting changed, just kicked off my shoes and lay there. Leaving just me and my thoughts.

'What happened?' How did I get out? Did I slow them down?'

The questions looped, sharper each time, stabbing at the empty space in my memory. My stomach twisted until it hurt just to breathe.

I needed answers.

I needed someone to tell me what had happened while I was out cold. My eyes landed on the phone on my bedside table. My hand shook as I lifted the receiver and dialled Ivory's number. Her parents were usually asleep at this time — or at least that's what she told me.

"Hello?" crackled Ivory's voice over the phone.

"Ivory, what happened at the party?" I whispered.

"Well, basically after Randy had his allergic reaction you passed out, and that's when everyone went crazy because you had already passed out at school on Monday. Then I collapsed because I had a sugar crash, and someone's parents came, and they chased us."

"No way!"

"Yeah, and then Mateo and Avery carried you while grabbing my arm, and Addi dragged Randy. We got to a fence and then we had to jump over it."

"What?" I whispered harshly.

"Yeah, and we threw you over the fence."

"You what?" I hissed.

"Then they grabbed Addi, but Troy, seriously, Troy, he fly-kicked the parent in the chest."

My eyes widened in the dark. "You're joking."

Another voice cut through the static. Cold. Sharp.

"So you were at a party," said the voice. My mum's voice. Right there on the line.

"Not the library," came another voice. Ivory's mum.

Ivory and I both hung up and I pretended to sleep, but it was too late.

Chapter 14

Addison: Glass and Guilt

I quickly sprinted out of the car, my heart still racing. I took my heel off and held it against my chest as I climbed to the top of the tree next to my window. Barely sitting on the branch, I struggled to keep my balance as I leaned over and tried to open the window with one hand.

Locked.

"Shit," I whispered, looking down at how far away the ground was. I looked at the heel against my chest and then back at the window. I knew I was going to regret this, but it was my only option.

'This is going to hurt.'

I slammed the heel of the heel into the window. Glass shattered everywhere. I ducked, but a couple of pieces stabbed me in the arms. I winced. I kept smashing the window, hoping Mum wasn't home. I took a deep breath. "One, two, three," I whispered.

I vaulted through the tiny gap I made, glass catching in my dress, arms, and legs. I quickly ran to my mum's room, took off the dress and put it back in the wardrobe. I returned the one heel, hoping she wouldn't notice the other was missing. I got into my pyjamas and took off my make-up. The doorknob started rattling. I raced back to my bed and lay there, pretending to sleep. Not like my mum checked anyway. Then I realised my cuts were bleeding and there was still glass in my arms and legs. I bit down on my shirt so I wouldn't scream. I sat up and slowly pulled the first piece of glass out from my arm. I grimaced as blood started pouring out quickly. I grabbed a cloth and wrapped it around the cut, securing it with a hair tie just like Jenny had taught me. I took out the second piece, the pain even worse. By the third piece there were tears streaming down my face. I started just yanking out the pieces. It hurt like hell, but it was the quickest way. I winced as the pain got worse each time. It was hard to not scream, but I tried my best.

Then I finally had to take out the one from the lamp at the party. I pulled, but it was stuck. I bit down as hard as I could. Small drops of blood started to drip out.

"Mmhh," I said, biting down on my shirt. I made that noise when something hurt too much.

'Just do it.'

I pulled out the shard quickly.

I screamed in pain and started sobbing. But there was no time for that. I sat up despite the pain and wrapped a cloth around my leg and secured it, hoping my mum didn't hear anything. I tried to go to sleep, but the thought of almost getting caught or someone almost dying and it being all my fault made me feel sick.

Chapter 15

Julianna: The Great Escape

Lately, I have been stressed. Really stressed. Almost every day this week we had gotten detention, and I went to a party. When my parents found out, I got into so much trouble, and they grounded me even though our group was going to the roller-skate warehouse this week, so I had no choice but to sneak out.

My parents and my older sister, Kaelin, were working late as usual, and my older brother, Kai, is looking after me and my little brother and sister, Lyra and Jaxon. I told Lyra and Jaxon to stay on the lookout, and I said it was a game so I wouldn't have to bribe them. Then I got a pillow, dressed it in my clothes and made it look like I was sleeping. I grabbed my outfit, which was some chunky sneakers, a black shirt and blue jeans, and of course I wore my bracelet. I opened my window; the air was cold. I grabbed a rope that I had made out of old bedsheets.
That's when I saw the black convertible. I threw my makeshift rope out the window and carefully climbed down, hoping I wouldn't faint again. I had fainted once I got home every day this week.

'Why did it always happen to me?' I thought to myself as I climbed down from my two-storey house.

The distance down was scary, and my vision started to blur. I shook my head.

'No, I have to get down first. If I need to faint, I'll have to do it once I get to the ground.'

I made it down safely and I actually didn't faint. I sprinted towards the car and got in.

"Did you just... jump out your window?" asked Mateo.

"Yep," I said.

"What if you got hurt?" asked Ivory.

"I didn't really think it through."

"Anyway, next stop is Addison's house," said Mateo.

"You're acting like we're on a bus," said Avery, drawing in his sketchbook.

"I mean, we kind of are," I said.

"God damn it!" yelled Blake.

"Dude!" said Avery, "stop yelling."

"Yeah man!" said Mateo, "I'm driving!"

"Not my fault! Someone knocked me out in Boxing!" said Blake.

Ivory face-palmed, annoyed.

Chapter 16

Addison: The Night Everything Changed

Then the day that changed our lives came — Saturday. At night I got into my black jeans and black t-shirt. I snuck out my window from the second floor and fell into a bush. I quickly got up and saw my friends all in the black convertible. I climbed in and we blasted music, talked and had so much fun until we picked up Blaire. She started acting like it was her car and kept telling us to be quiet when we were talking.

Then Ivory snapped. "Blaire shut up or we'll kick you out of the car onto the streets and tell Mrs Lindsey that you didn't help us with the project."

Blaire didn't talk for the rest of the drive, while the rest of us had fun. When we got to the abandoned roller-skate factory, it was dark and had cobwebs everywhere. We split up into groups of three. No one wanted to go with Blaire and Blake, so they had to go together, and Blake wasn't going to be much help because he was still playing on his Game & Watch. At this point I don't think he even sleeps. We walked around and took photos on Ivory's Canon camera. The place was pretty boring, just broken conveyer belts and old roller-skates that never got delivered. We walked back to the front of the factory and that's where Julianna, Ivory and I found a giant bucket with a neat handwritten note which read:

"Guys, the ink on the note. It looks too new, for an old and abandoned factory," said Ivory.

"You're right," said Julianna.

"Yeah, it almost looks like wet ink," I said, leaning closer.

We looked into the bucket and the substance looked sticky and it was glowing neon green. It looked unnatural.

Then something exploded from the other side of the factory, and it looked like this side was about to do the same. We quickly backed away from it and tried to run back to the car, but the heavy metal front door was locked. The substance exploded.

I woke up a few hours later and saw Julianna still passed out, but Ivory was up.

"What happened?" I asked, coughing out dust.

My ears were ringing and there was dust in my mouth, hair and clothes.

"I don't know, but we need to get out of here," said Ivory.

We dragged Julianna and tried to find a way out. Then we saw Mateo, Randy, Avery, Blaire and Blake near a window.

"Come on, we need to get out of here!" said Mateo.

"This is your fault," said Blaire, pointing at Ivory.

"It's not her fault!" said Avery.

"It's no one's fault guys!" said Randy, not looking up from his Rubik's Cube.

Suddenly Mateo grabbed his jacket, wrapped it around his fist and punched the glass. It shattered with a deafening crack. Everyone went silent. His knuckles started to bleed, but it didn't look like he noticed. We all climbed out the window, picked up Julianna and carried her to the car. Well, everyone except for Blake, Randy and Blaire.

Julianna sat up abruptly. "What happened?"

"You passed out," I replied.

"Oh, thanks for getting me out, guys."

Mateo grinned, wild and unshaken. "Since we're here, let's have some fun!"

"What kind of fun?" asked Ivory warily.

"You'll see."

We dropped Blaire and Blake home first and ten minutes later, we pulled into a glowing drive-in movie theatre. Cars were lined up under the giant screen, neon lights buzzing, speakers crackling as the opening credits rolled for a new movie called *Splash*.

"Shh guys, it's starting," said Julianna.

The movie played. For a while we laughed and passed popcorn around. Everything was normal. But then the screen flickered. The sound cut. And before I could blink, everything went black.

Chapter 17

Ivory: The Morning After

I woke up the next morning, and my back was killing me. I groaned and realised I was still in the car. Everyone else was still there too. All passed out.

As I tried to sit up my hand brushed the window and the vines outside curled tighter around the frame like they were alive. I yanked my hand back and thought,

'Weird.'

"Guys, wake up!" I yelled. Everyone jumped up, startled.

"Some of us weren't sleeping," Randy muttered, fiddling with his Rubik's Cube. Weirdly, it clicked into place faster than I'd ever seen before, like his fingers had suddenly become twice as quick.

"Well, some of us were," Mateo groaned, stretching. A faint scorch mark smudged the car seat where his hand had been, but he didn't notice.

"Guys, I don't think I can move," said Addison.

"Same," said Avery as he cracked his neck while shutting his sketchbook. A half-finished dragon doodle on the page almost looked like it had shifted when I glanced at it, but when I blinked it was still.

"Does anyone remember what happened last night?" Julianna asked softly. Her hair was damp, though no one had seen her near water.

"We must've just passed out from the explosion," Addison said quickly. "That's all it was."

No one argued. We were too tired, too freaked out, and too desperate to pretend everything was normal.

But nothing about this felt normal.

Chapter 18

Addison: Something's Different

Throughout the drive home I kept telling myself that everything was normal, even though something inside me felt like it had changed and everything about this felt wrong. My thoughts spiralled. I couldn't stop thinking about the goo from my necklace and how it looked exactly the same as that substance in the factory. How the note saying 'Do not touch' looked way too new. The car braked abruptly. I looked outside. It was my house.

"Bye guys," I said.

"Bye," they replied.

I could tell they were all just as shaken as I was. I quickly got out of the car and climbed up the tree next to my bedroom window. I vaulted through my already smashed window into my room, shards of glass sticking into my clothes. I changed into my pyjamas and walked down the stairs as if I'd been at home the entire time. My mum was in the kitchen, making waffles and listening to James Taylor.

'Ugh. That's so dinosaur era.'

"Addison, go get the orange juice from the fridge and set the table," said my mum.

I really didn't want to set the table.

Sighing, I thought '*Do it yourself.*'

To my surprise she did it herself. I didn't even have to ask.

I ate my food quickly and went upstairs to my room to brainstorm some ideas for the project. Going to the factory was such a waste of time. We didn't even get to look around for five minutes before the chaos started. I brainstormed for a couple of hours and then I felt really thirsty.

'*I wish Mum would bring me water.*'

Suddenly she appeared, a glass of water in her hand. She handed it over and went back downstairs without saying a word.

Something weird was definitely going on.

Chapter 19

Julianna: The Last Straw

I woke up and realised I had slept through two of my alarms, not the beeping kind, but my little sister, Lyra, and my little brother, Jaxon. As I brushed my teeth and hair, I thought of what hairstyle I should wear today. That's when I decided to do the same hairstyle I did all the time. Just leaving my hair out, I put on my blue t-shirt and blue denim shorts, stepped into my shoes and bolted out the door. Then I ran back into the house to get my *Adventures of Cascade* book.

I jumped on the bus and that's when I saw Blaire.

I thought to myself *'Just try to ignore her Julianna.'*

There were Ivory and Addison. They smiled at me and I smiled back.

"Julianna, sit here," said Ivory, shifting to make some space for me. I sat down.

"Hey guys," I said.

"Hey," said Addison.

"We're just finishing our homework," said Ivory.

"Okay, all good," I said as I pulled *The Adventures of Cascade* out of my bag. I loved disappearing into that world.

"Hey dork."

I looked up and saw Blaire and her minions smirking at me.

"H–hi Blaire," I said.

She grabbed my wrist with her ice-cold hands, her bright pink nail extensions digging into my skin. I winced. Then I stood up, afraid she would try something with my bracelet.

"What's this?" asked Blaire, looking at my bracelet and moving my wrist around to see every angle.

"It's my bracelet," I said, trying to pull my hand back, but it was no use. Blaire's grip was too strong for me.

"Not anymore," said Blaire as she ripped the bracelet off my wrist.

My eyes went wide as I gawked at Blaire, my chest tightened, and my heart was racing. She always tried to make me feel small, but this time she took the bracelet — *my* bracelet. My throat felt hot, like I couldn't breathe, and I could feel my eyes fill with tears of rage.

"Give it back!" I yelled louder than I meant to. Everyone stared at us.

"Ooh, kitten's got claws!" said Blaire, laughing.

I was about to lunge at her when I felt a soft hand grab my shoulder. I turned around and saw it was Ivory's. She shook her head. She didn't have to say anything; her eyes said it all. They said, 'Julianna don't do it, you'll regret it.' I shook Ivory's hand from my shoulder. Usually I wouldn't, but this time my bracelet was involved. I lunged at Blaire, trying to grab the bracelet.

Then Geniessa, stuck her leg out and I tripped, hitting my head on the metal seat. I cried out. I bit my cheek trying to hide all of my pain as I curled into a ball, hoping it would help stop the pain. I cried silently, hoping no one would look at me.

"Julianna!" cried Addison as she came to my side and got me to sit up. I leaned against her and the seat. Barely conscious. Tears streaming down my face.

"Jules, are you okay?" asked Addison, brushing my hair off my wet cheeks.

"I'm fine," I said even though I clearly wasn't. I started hyperventilating.

Way too much was happening. My bracelet was taken, and now my head was bleeding. I was about to give up and let myself pass out.

Until Addison said, "Julianna don't let Blaire win," as she tried to lift my head. I could feel blood dripping down the back of my head and onto my neck, warm and sticky. I nodded shakily. Then I winced. The back of my head throbbed. My eyes began to close but I tried to hold on for as long as I could. My vision was getting blurry from my tears. Addison wiped them for me, and I tried to smile. I turned back to Blaire.

Mateo stood up.

"Give me the bracelet!" he yelled.

"I'd rather not," said Blaire.

He tried to get the bracelet, but Blaire threw it to the front of the bus. Mateo went to the front of the bus and grabbed the bracelet. He knelt down beside me.

"I moved because I'm scared of what Ivory's about to do," said Mateo, making an effort to smile as he tried to tie the bracelet around my wrist. I smiled. Ivory would always protect me, no matter what. That's what she would say to me. Ivory stared at Blaire for a whole minute. She didn't say or do anything.

"What are you going to do? Stare me to death?" asked Blaire as her and her minions started cackling.

"Avery, bring me my bag now," said Ivory, her voice dark. I had never heard her like that before. She sounded like she was about to kill.

Avery didn't question her; he brought her bag over. Then he ran and hid behind us. "I have no idea what she's about to do."

Ivory pulled out a mini metal baseball bat and tossed her bag to the side. It landed with a thud. Then she gripped the bat tightly with both hands. Everyone gawked.

"Holy..." someone whispered, but they were interrupted by Ivory slamming the baseball bat onto the metal seat. The seat dented and made a sound like a gunshot. Everyone flinched. The bus driver, Gary, was blasting music, so he didn't hear anything. By now everyone in the bus other than our group and Blaire and her minions were leaning against the back window. No one made a sound.

Ivory twirled the bat as if it were a skipping rope. Then she smirked. "Princess Blaire, it's nap time," she said, mockingly sing-song.

"You're a freak!" yelled Blaire.

"Only when someone hurts my best friend," said Ivory in a dark and menacing tone.

Ivory swung the bat at Blaire's legs, knocking her to the ground. Blaire yelped as she hit the floor hard and then she passed out.

"Now, who's next?" asked Ivory with a huge smile, twirling the bat. Blaire's minions backed away from Ivory.

"Geniessa's next!" yelled Mateo, looking pissed.

"Geniessa, it's sleep time," said Ivory.

Geniessa tried to run but there was nowhere to go. Ivory hit her on the hip. Geniessa screeched as she collapsed and fell hard on her arm. Ivory did the same to Larissa and Clarissa, before kneeling next to me. She held my hand. It was warm and made me feel safe, completely the opposite of when Blaire grabbed my wrist. I gave her a small smile.

"I'm so sorry I let them hurt you," said Ivory, tears forming in her eyes.

"Yeah, me too," said Mateo.

"Me three," said Addison.

"Same," said Avery.

Randy finally looked up from his Rubik's Cube. "You dented the seat. Bus driver's gonna be pissed."

"You guys are the best!" I said, my words slurring. The world tilted, darkening. My last thought before blacking out: Ivory wasn't just my best friend. She was a storm.

Chapter 20

Ivory: And Then There Was Silence

Julianna passed out.

"Jules! Wake up!" I begged.

"We need to get her to the hospital!" yelled Addison.

We dragged her to the front of the bus and that's when bus driver, Gary, realised there were four more unconscious girls on the floor and thirty kids at the back of the bus screaming and crying. He took us straight to the hospital. They had to get Julianna into surgery because she'd cracked the back of her head.

I sat in the waiting room, fiddling with my necklace and trying not to cry. Avery sat down next to me. He handed me a creamy vanilla milkshake from the cafe. My favourite.

"She's going to be okay," said Avery, trying to cheer me up.

"Are you sure?" I asked.

"Yep," said Avery, taking a sip from his chocolate milkshake. "They're just going to stitch up her head".

"That's not reassuring at all."

"Yeah, but I can't believe you just pulled out the baseball bat."

I smirked. "I told you I would need it to protect us one day."

He laughed "I still can't believe that happened, my little sister pulling out a baseball bat and standing up to the worst bully in our school."

"We're twins!" I yelled as I gave him a playful punch in the shoulder. We both started laughing. It was the only good thing that had happened today.

Then Addison, Mateo and Randy walked into the waiting room. Addison kept fiddling with her hair, looking scared, Mateo kept glancing back and Randy was still playing with his Rubik's Cube.

"Julianna just went into surgery," said Addison.

"Does she have to stay in the hospital afterwards?" I asked.

"Only for a day," said Mateo.

I let out a sigh of relief. Then I looked at Randy. He was still trying to solve his Rubik's Cube. He hadn't looked up the entire time. Not once — not even when Julianna hit her head or when she passed out. It's like he just didn't care about anything other than the Rubik's Cube.

"Seriously, Randy?" I said.

He looked at me, annoyed. "What?"

"Julianna just went into surgery and you're playing with a stupid cube!" I yelled.

The barista stopped making coffee to watch the drama and a bunch of people stopped to stare at us.

"So?" he said.

"What did you just say?" I said, standing up I reached for my bag.

"Ivory, calm down," said Avery, grabbing my wrist.

I looked around at all the people staring at us. I reluctantly sat back down.

"Yeah, listen to your big brother," said Randy mockingly.

"We're twins," said Avery defensively.

"Who cares?" said Randy as he walked over to the cafe.

An hour passed. I jumped every time a nurse came into the room, hoping they would tell me that Julianna was awake.

'Please let her be alright,' I wished silently.

Avery gave me a hug. It's like he could read my mind. I looked over at Addison. She looked terrified, and to be honest I was too.

The thoughts kept rushing through my brain.

'What if something bad happened to Julianna? What if she lost too much blood?'

My heart began to race and my legs started to shake.

"BANG!"

We all turned as the doors burst open. A nurse came running toward us. She looked like she was going to give us good news.

"You guys are waiting for Julianna, right?" asked the nurse.

I smiled "Yeah, we are."

"We have some news about her," said the nurse.

She didn't sound sad so Julianna must have been okay. I was glad.

"What's the news?" I asked happily.

"We lost her," said the nurse.

My whole world shattered.

"What?" I whispered, tears streaming down my face.

"She lost too much blood. I'm so sorry," said the nurse.

Chapter 21

Addison: The Waiting Game

We had been in the waiting room for half an hour. I was terrified. Even though I only met Julianna a few days ago, she felt like my sister. Ivory definitely felt the same. Nurses and patients kept coming out of the operating room. I don't know why, but I had a bad feeling that Julianna wasn't going to be okay.

'You can't think like that,' I told myself.

"How long do you think she'll be?" I asked.

"Hopefully another twenty minutes," said Mateo, checking the clock on the wall.

I kept tapping my foot on the ground, hoping that it would somehow make time go faster. Randy came back and slumped down in the seat next to me.

"Far out, it took me half an hour just to get a damn coffee."

"Randy, shut up," said Mateo, not looking away from the operating room door. He sounded mad but looked worried at the same time. Randy rolled his eyes.

"I'm going for a walk," I said, standing up.

Mateo nodded, but he didn't take his eyes off the door. Randy went back to playing with his Rubik's Cube and acted like I wasn't even there.

Passing the operating rooms, the smell of antiseptic burned my nose and hearing those cries, the doctors delivering the bad news, it made my stomach twist. I needed to do something to relax. That's when I saw a florist shop with bluebells in the display window.

'Perfect.'

I went in and bought a bunch of bluebells for Julianna. She deserved something pretty and blue just in case... but no, she has to make it. She has to.

I came back to my seat holding the bluebells and watched whatever was on MTV to get my mind off of everything. I fidgeted with the floral wrap.

"BANG!"

I looked up. Blaire wobbled out with a cast on her leg, limping over towards us dramatically. I know it sounds harsh, but I've broken my leg before and that's not how people limp.

"She ruined me!" yelled Blaire as she limped as fast as she could towards Ivory.

"Shhh," said Avery.

Blaire stopped in front of them. "Why should I!?" she yelled back.

"She's sleeping. Now if you don't want me to break that other leg of yours, I'd suggest you shut up before I make you," said Avery, his voice scarily calm.

Blaire gulped and walked away.

'She was still picking fights after getting hit with a mini metal baseball bat. What an idiot.'

Geniessa, Clarissa and Larissa walked out after her with casts all over them. As soon as they saw us, they ran as fast as they could, following Blaire to the emergency exit.

"Damn, they're scared of us," I said.

"Yeah, thanks to Ivory here," Avery chuckled.

Randy didn't respond and I really wanted to chuck his Rubik's Cube out the window. Mateo was still staring at the door.

"She's going to be okay, right?" I asked, just to have someone reassure me.

"I hope so Addison, I really hope so," said Mateo, not turning away from the door.

"Yes!" screamed Randy, startling all of us.

We all turned to look at him, startled, except for Ivory, who was deep asleep.

"I solved my Rubik's Cube," said Randy.

"Julianna's in surgery and you're still playing with that stupid cube?" I snapped.

Randy scoffed, "Oh please, Julianna passed out so many times last week I'm starting to believe Ms Patricia."

Mateo got up and punched him in the face. Randy's glasses broke and he hit the floor hard, passing out because of the impact. That's when I released his glasses didn't just break — they melted.

"Addison, can you go call the nurse?" said Avery.

I nodded and sprinted to the reception desk.

"Excuse me, someone just..." I tried to think of what to say without getting Mateo in trouble.

"Someone what?" asked the receptionist, lowering her magazine.

"Someone passed out on level two in the waiting room next to the operating room,' I said.

"Oh dear," said the lady, "that's the fourth time this week."

My eyes widened.

'Damn, four times?'

"Nurse to level two waiting room please," the receptionist said into the speaker. "Again," she added as she rolled her eyes.

99

I went back upstairs. Mateo was sitting back in his seat staring at the operating room door again. Randy was still on the ground. The nurses came soon after and took him to another room. Then I saw the Rubik's Cube on the floor. I picked it up and threw it out of the window as hard as I could. I let out a sigh of relief.

"That felt good," I whispered to myself.

Suddenly I heard someone sobbing. I turned around. It was Ivory.

Chapter 22

Ivory: Second Chances

"Ivory, it's okay," said a voice. Someone was shaking me. I opened my eyes and saw Avery. He looked worried.

"What's wrong?" he asked.

"J...Julianna... Sh... She's gone," I croaked before bursting into tears again.

Avery hugged me.

"Ivory, she hasn't come out of surgery yet," said Avery.

I pulled away from him.

"What?" I asked.

"Yeah, she should be out in five minutes though."

"Wait, but the nurse said she lost too much blood?"

"Ivory, you must have had a nightmare."

"Nightmare? But I wasn't sleeping."

"Actually, you slept for a while," said Addison as she sat next to me.

"I did?"

"Yep," said Addison and Avery together.

I wiped my tears with my sleeve.

"So, she might be, okay?" I asked.

"Yes, hopefully," said Avery.

"I feel so stupid," I said, brushing some of my hair off my wet cheek.

Addison hugged me. "We're all worried about her."

"Yeah, and that's not being stupid," said Avery.

"Yeah, being stupid is when Blaire comes to you for a rematch," said Addison.

I chuckled. "That would never happen."

"It did," said Avery.

"What?" I asked.

"While you were sleeping," said Addison.

"What an idiot!" I said.

Avery, Addison and I laughed.

"Where's Randy?"

"Mateo knocked him out after he was happy about solving the Rubik's Cube and he started shit-talking Julianna," said Addison.

"Not gonna lie, I would have done that with my baseball bat if I was awake."

"I know you would've," said Avery.

"BANG!"

The doors flew open, and a nurse ran towards us.

"Are you here for Julianna Kim?" asked the woman, nearly out of breath.

"Yes!" we all said together.

"She's in a coma," said the nurse. "Even one more hour definitely would have killed her, but we're not entirely sure if she will wake up."

"Can we see her?" asked Addison.

"Yes, but she's in a coma," said the nurse. "Would you like to see her?"

"That is literally what I asked," snapped Addison.

The nurse went quiet. "Well follow me then."

Addison, Avery, Mateo and I all followed the nurse to a hospital room.

"She's in here," said the nurse.

She opened the door and there she was. Julianna was sleeping peacefully. She was pale and didn't have her usual huge smile.

"Oh Jules," I whispered as I ran to hug her.

"Has anyone contacted her family yet?" asked Addison.

"Oh, not yet," said the nurse, as if it was something like getting a new bouquet of flowers to replace dead ones.

"What do you mean?" I asked, "we've been sitting here for what? An hour? And you still haven't contacted her parents?"

"Well, if it's so important contact them yourselves for god's sake" said the nurse, annoyed as she left the room.

"Well, who knows Julianna's parents' number?" asked Avery. "'Cause I don't."

"Not me," I said.

"Definitely not me," said Addison.

"I think I might know her brother's number," said Mateo.

He dialled Julianna's brother using the hospital phone. "Umm... hey your sister is... in the hospital... she just had head surgery," said Mateo. He hung up

"Seriously no 'hi, hello' just your sister almost died, had surgery and no one called you until now," said Avery.

"I panicked; her brother is scary," said Mateo.

"You didn't tell him she's in a coma," I said.

"Whoops," said Mateo.

"At this point call Randy's parents and say, 'Hi Mr and Mrs Ford, I knocked out your son for being a jerk, he's in the hospital now," said Avery.

Addison spat out her water and started coughing.

"Careful, we don't want someone else staying in the hospital," I said, patting Addison's back.

"Yeah, at this point a third of our group is in the hospital for actually getting hurt," said Mateo.

A man and a woman in scrubs burst into the room.

Julianna's parents.

"Julianna!" yelled her mum.

"*Museun il-i il-eonass-eo!?*" demanded her dad.

"What happened!?" demanded her dad, louder this time.

"A girl called Blaire Pembroke pushed her onto a metal seat and she cracked her head open," said Addison.

"Yeah, she just had head surgery," said Mateo.

Suddenly her older brother Kai and her older sister Kaelin burst in. Kai looked like Julianna would if she were a boy, and Kaelin looked like an older version of Julianna.

"*Museun il-i il-eonass-eo*" asked Kaelin shakily.

"*Jullíananeun meoli susul-eul bad-assda*" said her mum, who was now crying.

"*Geuligo amudo uliege malhaji anh-assnayo!?*" snapped Kaelin.

Avery, Addison, Mateo and I all shot each other confused looks.

"We should probably go," muttered Avery.

We walked out of the room and went back to the waiting room.

"Who were those people?" asked Addison.

"The two doctors are her parents, and the two other people are her older siblings," I said.

"Hang on, I'm calling Randy's parents," said Avery. He used the hospital phone, and we watched him, wondering how he would break the news.

"Hi Mrs Ford, it's Avery. Randy had an accident and he's in the hospital now and..." Avery paused and took the phone away from his ear. "She hung up on me."

"Is Randy still passed out?" I asked.

"Let's go check," said Addison.

We asked the nurse which room he was staying in and she took us there. He was still unconscious, but this time no one was crying. He did this to himself. Only he was sleeping too peacefully after getting knocked out. It's like he was faking it. He was lying there with an oxygen clip on his finger like some tragic hero when really, he just got decked for being a jerk with a Rubik's Cube.

I rolled my eyes. "This jerk is taking up a hospital bed for being stupid while Julianna is fighting for her life."

Avery smirked, but it didn't last long. All of us were too scared to laugh. Mateo was pacing around looking like he'd punch the next person who walked in, and Addison was fiddling with the floral wrap while the bluebells shook, just like her hands. Avery pulled out his sketchbook and started sketching quickly.

"BANG!"

The door flew open. Randy's mum and older sister ran in.

"What happened!?" yelled his mum.

"He passed out," said Avery, not looking up from his sketchbook.

"Why are you so calm about it?" asked his sister.

"Because he deserved it," muttered Mateo.

"Excuse me!?" yelled his sister.

"Yeah, our other friend was having head surgery, and he said he didn't care," I said.

Randy's sister looked around and then suddenly stopped, her face white as a ghost.

"You did it, you little cow!" yelled his sister.

She slammed into me, knocking me onto the cold tiles with a loud thud. I cried out from under her weight. I scrambled for my bat, but she kicked it out of reach, the metal banging across the tiled floor. I swung a hand up to slap her, but she caught my wrist and twisted it until pain shot through my arm. My other hand was crushed beneath her heel. I cried out again, louder this time, half pain, half fury. Avery came and punched her right in her nose. She yelped as she fell backwards. Addison helped me up.

"What's wrong with you!?" yelled Avery.

"She hurt him!" yelled Randy's sister pointing at me.

"No, I did," said Mateo calmly.

"But she has a bat!"

"I used my fists," said Mateo calmly, as if he was reporting the weather.

"But... but..." started Randy's sister.

"But what?" I asked, out of breath.

"You're still a cow!"

"Come on let's go," said Addison.

She pulled me away and we went back to the waiting room. Julianna's family was there too.

"Hello," said Kaelin.

"Hi," I said, catching my breath.

"We have a problem," said her mum.

"Is Julianna okay?" I asked.

"Hopefully," said Kaelin.

"The nurse said that they need someone Julianna knows well to stay with her, but me and Julianna's dad have work so we can't stay with her," said Julianna's mum.

"I also have work," said Kaelin.

"I have to look after our other siblings," said Kai.

"So, we need one of you to stay with her if that's alright," said Julianna's dad.

"I'll stay," I said.

"Thank you," said Julianna's mum as the whole family left.

"Yeah, you're not staying by yourself, so I'll stay with you." said Avery.

"I'll stay too," said Mateo.

"Same," said Addison.

I nodded. "Okay. Then we'll take turns. Two-hour shifts. Someone's always with her."

Avery leaned back, folding his arms. "I'll start. Ten to midnight."

"I'll take last," said Mateo.

"I'll do second then," I said.

"I guess I'll do third," said Addison.

"What time is it right now?" asked Avery.

"I'll check." said Mateo "Damn, it's one o'clock"

"Let's go get some lunch," I said.

"What should we get?" asked Addison.

"Pizza," said Avery.

We all went to the cafeteria and got some pizza.

After he finished his food, Avery started sketching. He was drawing a bird. Suddenly it blinked at me, and I jumped up.

"What's wrong?" asked Addison.

"Avery y-y-your bird i-it just blinked at me," I said.

He looked down at the book. "It's not moving."

"Ivory, it's fine, you're probably just tired," said Addison.

"Yeah," I said, even though that's not what I wanted to say. Something just blocked me from saying it.

After a few hours we went to sit in Julianna's room to make sure she was okay. She had a bandage wrapped around her head.

"She looks so peaceful," said Addison as she put the bluebells on the side table and adjusted them.

"Yeah," I said.

Suddenly, Julianna's fingers began to curl. We all leaned in closer. Her eyes started to twitch.

"She's waking up," I whispered, relieved.

Her eyes opened slowly, and she gave us a small smile.

"Why do you guys look like you've been crying?" asked Julianna, her voice fragile but teasing.

We all started laughing, half amused and half relieved. Our Julianna was back. I exhaled for what felt like the first time all day.

"I'm so glad you're okay."

Julianna's smile widened. "It takes a lot more than Blaire and her hyenas to get rid of me."

She tried to sit up. We helped her as she leaned against the wall behind the bed. Her eyes started fluttering, like she was fighting to stay awake.

"Jules, you can sleep," said Mateo gently.

"Yeah, no one's leaving," I added.

She smiled. "Thanks guys."

She closed her eyes. I helped her lie down and brushed her hair out of her face. We sat in her room, silently watching her, all of us relieved. Our shining star, our beacon of hope and laughter, survived.

"BANG!"

The door slammed open and Julianna jolted awake.

"It's okay," said Addison, who was already sitting beside Julianna, holding her hand.

I turned to the door.

Randy.

He looked exhausted and lost without his Rubik's Cube.

"What do you want, Randy?" asked Avery.

"Another beating?" asked Mateo.

"No, I just wanted to apologise," said Randy.

"For what?" asked Julianna, confused.

"For umm... not being here," said Randy.

"No, that's not what you should be apologising for," snapped Mateo.

"She doesn't even know what happened. Let's keep it that way," said Randy.

"Well, she should know," said Mateo.

Julianna sat up properly. "What happened?"

Randy folded his arms. "Mateo knocked me out."

"Only because you were talking shit about Julianna," snapped Mateo.

"Yeah, Randy was being a jerk the entire time in the waiting room," I said.

Julianna didn't look surprised at all. She shrugged. "I never liked you from the start."

We all gawked at her.

"What?" asked Julianna "I'm just telling the truth, just like Randy likes to tell the truth about me."

"Okay, I am really sorry." said Randy.

"Why would you be sorry?" asked Julianna.

"Because you guys are the only people that I feel safe with," blurted Randy.

Avery stopped sketching. "What do you mean?"

Randy sighed. "My parents force me to practice being quick on my Rubik's Cube for more than eight hours a day. That's why I get six hours done at school and two on the bus ride back and forth. They ground me if I don't do enough hours. I didn't do eight hours yesterday and I've been on edge the whole time. That's why I lashed out."

His voice cracked halfway through. We all stared at him, wide-eyed.

"That's messed up," said Addison quietly.

"Yeah, well, it's my life," Randy muttered.

Mateo lowered his voice. "Still doesn't excuse what you said about Julianna."

"I know," said Randy. "I just... didn't know how to be normal around you guys."

We all looked around at each other, unsure if we should forgive him or not.

Julianna sighed. "I'll only forgive you if you stay still while they beat you up however they want."

We all looked at her in shock.

"Only if you guys want to," added Julianna.

Mateo cracked his knuckles and smirked. "Gladly."

We all beat him up. Not proper hitting, more like a playful beating. Except for Mateo, who went all out. I grabbed a pillow and smashed it in his face, Mateo jabbed him in the stomach, Avery slammed his head with his sketchbook and Addison pulled his hair. Julianna sat on the bed giggling softly.

"Come on guys, isn't that enough!?" cried Randy.

We all stopped hitting him and burst out laughing.

"Do any of you guys have Uno cards?" asked Julianna suddenly.

"I can go get some," said Mateo.

"Oh my god, this is going to be so much fun!" exclaimed Addison.

That's when I realised Julianna, Mateo, Avery, Randy and I always played Uno together, but we'd never played with Addison.

"I'll be back in ten minutes," said Mateo.

"I'll go get some food," said Avery.

"I'll go find my Rubik's Cube," said Randy.

All three of them left.

"I'm not telling him what happened to the Rubik's Cube," said Addison.

"What happened to it?" asked Julianna, already smiling.

"I threw it out the window."

"He's not going to be happy."

"He won't find out," I said as I sat on the edge of Julianna's bed. Addison sat next to me.

"Can you guys fill me in on everything?" asked Julianna.

"Of course," I said. "First you passed out and bus driver Gary drove us to the hospital. Then we waited and I yelled at Randy for playing with his Rubik's Cube."

Julianna laughed. "I'm not surprised."

"Yeah," said Addison, "but then Blaire came to Ivory for a rematch and Clarissa, Geniessa and Larissa were all scared of us."

"Wait, so did Blaire get a rematch?" asked Julianna.

"Nope," said Addison "Ivory was sleeping and Avery threatened Blaire."

"Damn," said Julianna, grinning.

"And then Mateo knocked Randy out and the nurse told us you were in a coma," said Addison.

"After that, Mateo called your brother and the rest of your family came," I said.

"And then Ivory got into a fight with Randy's older sister," said Addison.

"What!?" exclaimed Julianna.

"Yeah, that was all you missed," I said.

"Why do I miss the craziest things!?" asked Julianna.

The door creaked open.

"I got the Uno cards," said Mateo.

"And I got some food," said Avery.

"Where's Randy?" I asked.

"Looking for his cube," said Avery, taking a bite out of his sandwich.

"He's not going to find it," said Julianna in a sing-song voice.

"Yeah, a bird probably took it by now," said Mateo.

"What's a bird going to do with a Rubik's Cube?" asked Avery.

Addison smiled. "Make it into a nest."

We all burst out laughing.

We pulled up some chairs and used Julianna's bed as a table.

Mateo shuffled the cards like he was a Vegas dealer. The first few rounds were surprisingly calm, until Addison forgot to say 'Uno' three times in a row, Avery kept trying to peek at my cards, Mateo narrated every move like a sports commentator and Julianna laughed so hard she had to hold her stomach.

"Avery, pick up four," I said as I put down a plus four.

"Nope," said Avery. "Addison pick up eight."

"What!? You can't stack those!" exclaimed Addison.

"House rules," said Avery calmly.

"You've been waiting the entire game to use that," said Mateo.

"Strategic patience," Avery said, grinning.

"Strategic betrayal," muttered Addison, drawing her cards dramatically.

We all cracked up.

"Mateo, draw four," said Julianna.

"No thanks," said Mateo as he put down a plus two.

"You can't stack a plus two on a plus four!" yelled Addison.

"Since when?" asked Mateo.

"Since always! It's literally on the box!" I yelled.

"Well, where's the box?" asked Mateo.

"You threw it out, genius!" yelled Avery.

Julianna started laughing and crying tears of laughter at the same time. Then the real chaos started. Everyone started screaming.

"Who keeps switching it back to red?" yelled Mateo.

"You can't play that card!" yelled Avery.

"Avery! Stop looking at my cards!" I yelled.

"Who shuffled these?" asked Julianna.

"Draw two, enjoy!" said Addison.

"UNO!" yelled Avery.

"Someone change the colour!" exclaimed Julianna.

"Don't worry Jules. I'm not letting him win that easy," said Mateo. Smirking, he put down a plus four.

"You do know that's going to Ivory and not me, right?" said Avery.

Mateo folded his arms and leaned back on his chair with a confident smile. "I know."

I slammed a plus four on the pile.

"I'm not picking up eight," said Addison as she put a plus four down.

"You're all teaming up on me!" exclaimed Avery.

Julianna grinned as she put her plus four down.

Avery sighed as he ran a hand through his hair "How many?"

We all started mentally calculating.

Julianna smiled sweetly "Sixteen."

We all burst out laughing while Avery started drawing cards.

"I can't even hold that many!" exclaimed Avery.

Mateo had two cards left and he stacked a blue seven and a yellow seven. "Boom!" he said.

"Damn it," whispered Addison.

I turned to the clock

"Guys, it's midnight."

Avery looked at the clock. "Damn."

Addison started shuffling the cards "Okay, last round, winner takes all."

Mateo raised an eyebrow "What's 'all'?"

I smirked. "Bragging rights."

Julianna chimed in, "And the last sandwich!"

"Umm..." said Avery, "I already ate it."

"Avery!" we all yelled.

Everyone wanted to win. The game was intense.

"Whose turn is it?" asked Julianna.

"How am I on fourteen cards already!?" exclaimed Addison.

"Draw four!" said Mateo.

Julianna picked up four cards dramatically.

"I'm changing it to green!" I said.

"You skipped me twice, Avery!" yelled Addison.

"Ivory, you forgot to say Uno!" said Julianna.

"Ivory, pick up two!" said Mateo.

"Did the devil shuffle this deck?" asked Addison.

"Yeah, we need to call an exorcist," said Avery.

"Plus two Jules!" I said.

"That was mean," said Julianna as she put down a plus four.

"Plus four!" shouted Mateo, slamming his plus four on the pile. Right at that moment an angry-looking nurse came in.

"Shh!"

We all ignored her.

"Payback time," said Addison as she played two plus fours.

"Nice try," said Avery as he played a plus two.

"You guys are the worst!" I said as I picked up twenty cards. At this point I couldn't even hold my cards.

Mateo looked at Julianna and started laughing. "Jules stop smiling like that! You're up to something!"

"I'm not," giggled Julianna, still smiling funnily.

I started laughing. "Julianna, you laugh like that when you lie!"

Julianna giggled again. "No I don't."

Mateo started laughing again. "You did it again!"

Addison smiled, "Yeah Jules, you don't have to hide it."

"Okay then…" said Julianna, "PLUS TWELVE!" She slammed three plus four cards.

"You've got to be kidding me," said Addison.

"Sorry Addi," said Julianna, still smiling.

Addison started picking up twelve cards.

"Change to red!" said Avery.

"Back to blue!" said Julianna.

"Yellow!" said Mateo.

"Green!" I said.

"Yellow again!" said Addison.

"Red!" said Avery.

"Uno!" yelled Julianna as she played a red three, "and boom!" she said as she put a blue three on top.

"Guys," I said, "It's twelve thirty."

"That one round went on for thirty minutes?!" exclaimed Avery.

"Jules, you should sleep," said Mateo.

"Yeah, otherwise you might not be able to leave the hospital tomorrow," added Addison.

"Okay, goodnight, guys," said Julianna.

She fell asleep as soon as her head touched the pillow. I wished I could fall asleep that fast.

"Okay, since we're all up we don't even have to take turns until we get really tired," I said.

They all nodded. We watched over Julianna, watching her chest rise and fall, using the corridor light seeping in to see her without waking her up. I wasn't paying attention to anything but her.

"Hey," whispered Addison.

I flinched and turned around. She was sitting next to me, and Avery and Mateo had fallen asleep sitting up.

"What's up?" I whispered.

She leaned in. "Does Ravenwood air eat pictures?"

I leaned closer. "What? No."

She took off her locket and opened it. There was a photo of her and two girls, an empty gap between two of them. I looked at her, confused.

She sighed. "This might sound crazy, but there used to be four people in this photo."

My eyes widened in the dark "What?"

She swallowed hard. "Yeah, there was a brunette, a redhead, a blonde and me."

"But how do you know it was because of Ravenwood air?"

"Because on the first day of school I looked at it and the redhead was gone."

"What if the picture was just old?"

"They just got it for me two weeks ago."

"That's so weird."

"Yeah, and it was after I saw a sticky green goo on it."

"Wait, I found a sticky green goo on my necklace last week as well."

"You did?"

"Yeah. When we have gym class, we have to take off our jewellery and when I found it in my locker there was green goo on it."

"Something's not right," said Addison.

Chapter 23

Addison: Game On

After that conversation with Ivory, I couldn't stop thinking about the goo. How I had overlooked it so easily and how the exact same thing happened to her. But the question that stuck with me the entire night was:

'What if it had happened to Julianna too?'

We were still in Julianna's room. It was eight a.m. and Julianna was still asleep. We were sitting on the hospital chairs and eating — you guessed it: sandwiches.

"What time do you think they'll let her leave?" asked Ivory.

I took a bite from my sandwich. "I'm not sure."

Mateo got up to throw his sandwich wrapping in the bin. "Hopefully as soon as possible."

Julianna sat up and stretched her arms. She rubbed her eyes. "What time is it?"

"It's eight o'clock," said Avery.

She yawned. "Do I have to go to school today?"

"No way," said Mateo.

"Yeah, and we're skipping school to stay with you!" said Ivory, excitedly.

"So, what should we do today?" asked Julianna.

"You need to rest, Jules" I said.

"I know," said Julianna, "but can we still do something fun?"

"Let's play Guess Who!" said Ivory.

"I'll go find a board," said Mateo.

"It's fine, I'll just take a cab home and get mine. Me and Ivory already made a custom one of our grade in Year 8. I'll just add a picture of Addison," said Avery.

"Okay, let's go," said Mateo.

They both left.

"So, we should probably do teams," said Ivory.

"Boys versus girls?" I suggested.

"Yep." said Julianna.

We waited for about twenty minutes and that's when Mateo and Avery came back.

"What took you so long?" asked Ivory.

"Finding a picture of Addison," said Avery.

"Where did you find a picture of me?" I asked.

"On Ivory's camera from the warehouse," said Avery.

"Let's play!" said Julianna.

We set up the board using Julianna's bed as the table.

"Okay, let's start," said Mateo.

"Who asks first?" asked Ivory.

"Ladies first," said Mateo.

We all cracked up. Our card was *Troy*.

'We can't make it too obvious.'

"Is your person a boy?" asked Julianna.

"Nope," said Avery.

"Is your person a boy?" asked Mateo.

"Yep," said Ivory.

"Does your girl have blonde hair?" I asked.
"Nope," said Mateo.
"Does your boy have brown hair?" asked Avery.
"Yes," said Ivory.
"Does your girl have brown hair?" asked Julianna.
"Yes," said Mateo.

'Okay brown hair, could be me or someone from Blaire's group, or just a random student.'

"Is your boy Mateo?" asked Avery.
"Nope," said Ivory.
"Why would it be me?" asked Mateo.
"It's a boy with brown hair," said Avery.
"So?"
"Guys," said Julianna, "Chill."
"Okay, is your girl part of Blaire's group?" I asked.
"Yes" said Avery.

'So, Larissa or Geniessa, because Clarissa has ginger hair.'

"Is your boy in Year 8?" asked Mateo.
"Yes," said Ivory.
"Is your girl Geniessa?" asked Julianna.
"Dammit," said Avery.
Mateo sighed, "Yeah, it is."
"Who did you guys get?" asked Avery.
"Troy," I said.
"You should have said the fly-kick boy," said Mateo.
We all burst out laughing.
Randy walked in.
"Hey guys can I join you?" asked Randy.
"Sure," said Avery.
"Okay, round two," said Julianna.

Our card was *me*.

"Is your person a boy?" I asked.
    "Nope," said Avery.
    "Is your person a girl?" asked Mateo.
    "Yes," said Julianna.
    "Is your person blonde?" asked Ivory.
    "Nope," said Randy.
    "Is your person careful?" asked Avery.
    "No way," I said.

'Completely the opposite in fact.'

"Is your person kind?" asked Julianna.
    "Definitely," said Mateo.

'So, it's not Blaire or her group.'

"Is your person crazy?" asked Randy.
    "Kind of," said Ivory.

'Wow. She thinks I'm crazy!?'

"Okay, big hint time," said Mateo.
    "I'll give our hint," I said.
    "Can I give the hint from our team?" asked Randy.
    "Sure," said Avery.
    "Okay, our person is amazingly cool," I said.
    "Ivory?" asked Avery.
    "Julianna?" Mateo
    "Blaire?" asked Randy.
    They all looked at him with confusion.
    "What?" asked Randy. "It was just a guess!"
    "Did me or Avery get it right?" asked Mateo.

"Neither of you did," I said.

'I was joking about the cool part. Hehe they'll never get it.'

"Okay, I'll give our hint," said Randy. "Our person faints way too much."

Mateo jabbed him in the stomach and Avery slammed his sketchbook on his head.

"Me!" said Julianna happily.

She said it as if Randy hadn't just insulted her in the worst way.

"Yeah, it was you," said Mateo.

"Okay, but who was the amazingly cool person?" asked Avery.

"It was Addison," said Ivory.

"Oops," said Avery. "Sorry."

"It's all good," I said. "Let's play one last round."

Our card was *Avery.*

"Is your person a girl?" asked Ivory.

"Yes," said Avery.

"Is your person a boy?" asked Mateo.

"Yep," said Julianna.

"Is your person annoying?" I asked.

"Yes," said Randy.

"No," said Avery at the exact same time.

They looked at each other. Avery punched him in the stomach.

"Oww!" cried Randy.

"So, no?" I asked

"Yep," said Mateo.

"Is your person protective?" asked Avery.

"Yes," said Ivory.

"Is your person short?" asked Julianna.

"Yeah," said Mateo.

"Okay, big hint time," said Julianna.

"I'll give it," said Ivory.

"And I'll give ours," said Avery.

"Our person loves art," said Ivory.

"Blaire?" Randy asked

"Bro, you wasted our turn," said Mateo.

"Whoops," said Randy.

"Our person loves plants," said Avery.

"Me?" said Ivory.

"Randy, look what you did!" said Avery.

"Who did you guys get?" asked Randy.

"Avery," said Ivory.

"We win again," I said.

"Yep, the girls are undefeated," said Julianna.

"Yeah, but if you had Randy on your team then you wouldn't be winning," muttered Avery.

There was a knock on the door.

"I'll get it," said Ivory.

It was a nurse. "Miss Julianna Kim, you have to sign this. Your parents already signed the guardian section."

"Okay," said Julianna. She signed her name on the paper, her hands trembling slightly.

"You're free to leave anytime within the next three hours," said the nurse, "but you have to let the secretary know first."

Julianna smiled. "Okay."

The nurse left the room.

Ivory sat on the edge of Julianna's bed. "So, when do you want to go?"

"We can go now," said Julianna. "You guys can come over to my house if you're allowed to."

"Yeah, let's just get a cab home" I said.

Julianna got up, her legs shaking. We all supported her and brought her down to the reception desk. They made her sit in a wheelchair, even though she swore she could walk.

Ivory started to pin her hair up with a flower pin. "I'll push you."

"No, I'll push her," said Mateo.

"No, I want to," I said.

"No, me," said Avery.

Suddenly Mateo ran and pushed the wheelchair before any of us could, grinning like it was a race car.

"Hey! Come back!" yelled Ivory as she bolted down the corridor, chasing after him, her hair unravelling. She was surprisingly fast.

"Wait for me!" I yelled, chasing both of them.

Julianna sat in the chair, laughing, her hair flying back as Mateo sped around corners.

"Wait guys!" yelled Avery. "It's not easy holding a whole Guess Who board, my sketchbook and the Uno cards!"

Randy trailed behind, shaking his head like he'd seen this chaos a thousand times before.

Chapter 24

Ivory: Fast Lane

I ran after them, half for fun and half to get to push Julianna around. She's *my* best friend after all. That's when I saw it. A medical cart. I grabbed and pushed off just like you would on a skateboard. You see, when I was twelve, I got a skateboard, and I loved it — until I fell off and broke my arm. This time it was safer.

Probably.

I sat, one leg on the cart and the other on the floor ready to push. I built up momentum and tried to turn using my leg on the floor.

"Stop!" yelled a nurse.

I didn't listen. I didn't need to. I kept building up speed until I was next to them.

Mateo turned his head. "What the hell!?"

Julianna just kept laughing.

I kept my balance using one arm, the other reaching for the wheelchair. The cart kept swerving. My leg almost caught in the wheelchair's wheels.

Mateo started running faster. He was a lot quicker than me.

"Shit," I whispered.

"Ivory!" yelled Addison.

I turned around. Addison was running right behind me.

"Jump on!" I yelled.

She vaulted on.

"I'll push with my leg on the left you do it on the right," said Addison. We built up twice as much speed in half the time. It felt like we were flying. When we got near them again, Addison stuck her arm out, reaching for the wheelchair's seat. Suddenly the cart swerved. Addison yelped. She was hanging on to the chair by the back of the seat, shaking, her legs barely missing the ground.

'Shit. If her leg touches the ground at this speed...'

"Mateo, stop the wheelchair!" I yelled.

"I can't! I built up too much speed!" he yelled back.

While I was distracted the cart turned, and all that was in front of me was a potted plant and a wall. I closed my eyes, bracing myself for the hit. Suddenly I was lifted off the cart.

By a huge plant.

My eyes jerked wide open. Avery caught up to us. Mateo slowed down the wheelchair as quickly as he could. Addison put her foot on the ground and got off.

"Ivory, where did that tree come from?" asked Avery.

"I-I don't know" I said, still shaken. I thought I was going to die, but the thing I had looked after all my life was the thing that saved me. I slowly got off the plant and stepped on the floor.

"Hey! You kids!" yelled a nurse.

"Looks like that's our cue to go," said Addison.

We all bolted. Even Randy was running this time.

We ran outside the hospital, all of us gasping, panting and laughing.

"We're going to be banned for life!" exclaimed Avery, still holding the Guess Who board, sketchbook, and the Uno cards.

We all laughed.

But there was still a thought stabbing the back of my mind.

'How did that plant grow and lift me?'

"Guys, it's one o'clock," said Addison.

"Let's go get lunch!" said Mateo.

We walked to a nearby cafe with bright pink and blue seats and neon lights glowing, there was a line of arcade machines along the back wall. We sat at an empty booth.

"Wow, the places here are very..." said Addison looking for the right word.

"Bright?" asked Avery.

"Yeah."

We started looking through the menu. The waitress, a girl about our age, came up to us.

"Hi, what would you like?" she asked.

"I'll take a black coffee and a meat pie," said Avery.

"I'll have a white coffee and a chicken sandwich," said Mateo.

"I'll have a chocolate milkshake and a cheese sandwich," said Julianna.

"I'll take an iced coffee and a meat pie," said Addison,

"I'll take a black coffee and a mayo sandwich," said Randy,

"I'll have an orange juice and a meat pie," I said.

"Okay," said the girl as she walked away.

Avery and Mateo looked at each other and then at the forks and spoons. Then they grinned. They started to balance the forks and spoons on top of one another.

Julianna leaned over. "What?"

Addison crossed her arms. "Are?"

I slapped my face. "You doing?"

"We're making catapults," said Mateo.

"Call the waitress back," said Avery.

I stuck my hand up for her to come. She walked over.

"Yes?"

"Could we have some marshmallows?" said Avery.

"Certainly," said the waitress.

They grabbed some more spoons to add to the catapult.

"Here's your marshmallows," said the waitress.

"Ready?" said Avery.

"Yep," said Mateo.

Avery slapped the fork, which hit the spoon, making the marshmallow on the spoon fly straight into Mateo's mouth. while the spoon flew and hit a bald guy a few tables down right in the back of his head.

"Yes!" said Mateo and Avery in unison as they high fived.

The guy turned around and glared at us. Avery ducked behind his sketchbook — like that would help. Mateo didn't realise the guy was looking at him.

"Here's your food," said the waitress.

We all dug in straight away. Turns out after all that running you tend to get hungry.

Chapter 25

Ivory: Fall

We took Julianna home and stayed with her in her room, but what happened with the plant wouldn't leave me alone. I stood up.

"Jules, I got to go. I have so much Science homework."

'That was a lie'

"All good Ive," said Julianna.

I hugged her and left quickly. I needed alone time. I needed to think.

I went to Stereo Fever, my favourite record shop. I went there when I didn't want to go home. It was my safe place. Mick, the owner, was there as usual, ordering everything by genre and in alphabetical order. He was doing the Alternative Rock section. Claire, his twenty-year-old daughter, who also worked there, was restocking Madonna albums. She was like the big sister I never had.

"What's up Ivory," she said.

"Hey, Claire."

"Hi, Ivory," said Mick.

"Hey, Mick."

Avery and I basically grew up in this store and everyone knew who we were. I looked through the Alternative section, but nothing would get my mind off of what happened.

I went through the shop's back door to the back alley. Most people think that's where the criminals are, but I've never seen one there. I had the hood of my sweatshirt up, hiding my face. Just in case someone I knew walked past. I turned on my Walkman and put on my orange foam headphones. I listened to Wham! Most people didn't believe me when I said music and exercise helped me think, but it really does. I looked up at the brick wall. On the other side sat the most beautiful meadow I had ever seen. There were healthy trees everywhere, all the flowers you could imagine — and no one knew about it. Because no one came to this place *ever*.

I rolled up my sleeves and pulled the hood down. I wiped my sweaty palms and tucked my necklace under my sweatshirt. I grabbed at the tiny dents in the wall. They were almost unnoticeable. *Almost.*

My shoes slotted into the other hollows. I began to climb, sweat pouring down my face. Everything was good until I missed a foothold. My heart raced as I fell and barely grabbed onto the next dent with one arm, the rest of my body dangling. I gasped for air as I desperately tried to hoist myself back up. First my arm and then my two legs. My heart still hadn't slowed.

"Geez, Pearce, how are you this clumsy?" I muttered to myself.

After a couple of minutes, I was still climbing the wall, and that's when someone tugged me by my hood. I lost my grip. I reached out, trying one last time to save myself, but my palm was too sweaty and it ended up with a nasty scratch as it scraped against the wall. I fell on my side on the concrete. Hard. I cried out as pain flared up the side of my body.

"Look, Plant Girl's trying to leave," said a familiar voice.

I looked up and standing over me were Blaire and Geniessa. The rest of the minions had probably abandoned them by now. But for some weird reason, they weren't wearing their over-the-top and in-style clothes. Instead, they were in regular street clothes. Like they were trying to be discreet. Blaire's hood was on, and she looked not *as* mean as she usually did. She looked panicked.

"What's wrong?" said Geniessa. "The little shit didn't wake up and now you're escaping?"

I shot up and then realised that was probably the worst mistake I could have made. Pain stabbed my leg and I wobbled forward, barely keeping my balance. I could already see the purple and blue bruises on my legs. My hip was probably way worse.

"What happened to your cast?" I asked, out of breath. I remembered hitting them so hard that it was impossible for them to not break a bone.

"My dad's rich, don't you know that?" said Blaire. Her voice was usually mocking, but this time it just sounded monotone.

"She wouldn't," said Geniessa, crossing her arms. "The little shit wouldn't either."

I lunged at Geniessa, the pain still burning, but I didn't care. Julianna was more than my best friend. She was my sister.

"No one calls my best friend a little shit!" I yelled, half pain and half fury.

I landed on her, grasped her dark hair and yanked it as hard as I could. She shrieked. I'm not sure if it was the pain or the fact that her 'perfect' hair was being ripped out. I threw her ripped hair to the side. Blaire didn't try to step in. She knew nothing she could do would stop me in my rage. I headbutted Geniessa. It hurt a bit, but not as much as it hurt her. She screeched. I punched her in the face and her nose started to bleed.

She sprang up, knocking me to the ground. I hit the floor again, this time the back of my head hitting the floor first. Instantly the plants around me shot up. I ignored them and groaned as I forced myself to get up. I staggered to my feet, swaying a bit.

Blaire stepped forward. She grabbed something out of her shirt pocket. The worst thing she could ever pull out.

A knife.

I gulped. I was traumatised by knives. I stepped back cautiously.

"Blaire…" I said, my voice trembling, "put the knife down."

"Like how you put the bat down?" snapped Geniessa.

Blaire was almost in tears. I had never seen her like this before.

"Ivory," she whispered. It almost looked like she pitied me. "I'm sorry."

"Blaire, please" I whispered.

"If you won't do it I will!" threatened Geniessa.

Blaire froze. Geniessa snatched the knife from her and ran at me. I stumbled backwards, knocking over a few garbage cans. I grabbed the lid of one and used it as a shield. She stabbed the knife into the lid. It pierced the metal, almost stabbing me in the chest. I threw the lid at her, catching her off guard. I used that chance to tackle her. She dropped the knife and it clattered on the pavement, landing next to Blaire's sneaker.

"Blaire!" yelled Geniessa as she sat up. "Finish the job!"

I couldn't find the strength to get up.

Blaire picked up the knife hesitantly. Her hands were trembling.

"It's now or never, Blaire!" yelled Geniessa.

I looked at Blaire, my eyes begging her not to do it. She gave me an understanding look and exhaled. She tossed the knife at the bins and it disappeared into a rubbish bag.

I sighed, relieved.

"Geniessa, let's go," Blaire called out, already walking away.

Geniessa looked at me as I sat up and suddenly swung her fist and punched me right in the temple. Everything went black.

Chapter 26

Julianna: Torchlight

After everyone left I tried to sleep, but I just couldn't. Something was bothering me; something was wrong. That's when the phone rang. It was Addison. Her voice crackled.

"Jules, Ivory's missing."

I sat up. "What!?"

"Avery said she wasn't at home," said Addison.

I swallowed hard. "I'm coming."

"No Jules." said Addison. "It's too dangerous."

"I don't care. Ivory's my best friend."

"What if you faint?"

"I won't."

"What if you..."

I cut her off. "I won't. I promise."

I hung up. I changed and grabbed my bike and torchlight. It was getting late. We might not be able to find Ivory if it got darker.

I called out for her while riding past the arcade, the diner, and even the skate park. I asked the supermarket workers, the workers at the diner and Mrs Viola, the woman who owns the flower shop down the road.

I heard a voice from the distance. "Julianna!"

I turned and shone my torchlight. It was Addison. The rest of the group was there too, on their bikes. I rode over to them.

"Any luck yet?" I asked.

"No," said Addison.

"We're going to Stereo Fever next," said Avery.

We rode over to Stereo Fever, our favourite record store in Ravenwood, it was in the mall. Galaxy Plaza.

Avery pushed the door open. Mick, the owner, sat at the front counter, flipping through a magazine.

"Hey Mick," said Avery.

"Hey li'l dude," said Mick.

"Have you seen Ivory?"

"Yeah, she came in and looked at a few things. She looked… different."

"What do you mean, 'different'?" I asked.

"She looked kind of lost," said Mick.

"When did she leave?" asked Avery.

"About two hours ago, through the door to the back alley."

Avery's voice shook. "The back alley?"

"Yep."

Avery sprinted towards the door and bolted out.

"Avery! Wait!" yelled Addison as she chased after him.

Mateo and I ran, trying to catch up to them. Randy walked slowly behind us, skimming through the Electro section.

We made it outside. Avery and Addison were already looking around and calling out for Ivory.

"Why would Ivory go here?" asked Avery, running his hands through his hair.

"Probably because there's a whole meadow over the wall with trees and flowers. There's a lake there too," I said.

"Where?" asked Avery.

"There," I said as I pointed to the left.

"Let's go there," said Addison.

We ran, calling out for her. "Ivory! Ivory!"

No response. It was pitch black. All you could see were silhouettes of rubbish bins and whatever you would find in an abandoned alleyway and whatever the torches were lighting. There was a tipped over garbage bin with a hole through the lid. We could hear the faint sound of Wham! playing.

"We must be getting close," I whispered.

My shoe landed in a puddle and I almost slipped. I grabbed something to keep my balance.

"You okay?" asked Mateo.

"Yeah," I said.

He shone his torchlight to the floor.

"Blood," we both whispered.

"Avery!" Mateo called out.

Avery turned back. "What?"

"There's blood."

He ran back and looked at the blood. "Shit."

"Guys," said Addison, "I think there's something on the floor."

We turned. She was right. There was a silhouette of someone lying there. I shone my torchlight.

Ivory.

I ran to her. "She's bleeding," I said, panic cracking my voice.

Avery checked her pulse.

"She's alive," he said, relieved.

"We need to get her help," said Addison.

Randy walked over slowly, chewing gum and playing with his new Rubik's Cube. "Looks like someone picked the wrong fight."

"You better shut up before I make you," snapped Avery.

Ivory groaned.

"She's waking up," I whispered.

Her eyes opened slowly. She mumbled something I couldn't understand.

"Ivory?" asked Avery.

"Ave?" she whispered.

"Yeah, I'm here," Avery said softly.

"Knife."

We all shot Avery terrified looks. He ignored us.

"Where?"

Ivory slowly lifted her arm and pointed at a rubbish bag. "Th... there."

Her eyes were wide. She looked shaken. Of course, anyone with that many scars and bruises would be shaken.

"Let's get you home," said Avery.

Avery and I gently lifted Ivory up. She winced. We tried to lift her up more carefully.

"Put her on my bike, it's bigger," said Addison.

We gently sat her down on the bike's crossbar. Addison sat on her bike, gently balancing Ivory.

"Hang on to Addi, Ive," I said.

"Okay," mumbled Ivory as she leaned her head weakly on Addison's chest. Addison held onto the bike handle with one hand and Ivory's back with the other.

"Stay close, just in case," said Addison, turning her head towards us.

We nodded. Avery and I rode beside her, while Mateo and Randy stayed behind us. We started riding back to Ivory's house. The only light was coming from our bikes and a couple dim streetlights. My head began to throb, but I didn't say anything. I just held on for Ivory. Just like she had held on for me at the party.

Ivory kept sliding and Addison had to keep pushing her back, making her lose control of the bike for a couple of seconds. I was just glad that Ivory was okay. If she wasn't, I didn't know what I would do. The street started to blur, but I shook myself awake, focusing on the road ahead.

"You sure you're okay?" asked Mateo.

I turned. "Yeah, I'm fine."

"Where do we take her?" said Addison.

"To our house," said Avery "It's about twenty minutes from here. Do you think you can hang on?"

"I'll be fine," said Addison.

"Knife," Ivory kept mumbling.

She never told me anything about a knife. The back of my head felt like it was being stabbed. I blinked hard and everything went black.

Chapter 27

Addison: Cedar Way

There was a sudden crash. I turned around. Julianna passed out. "Jules!"

My bike skidded to a stop. Ivory clung to me. It made it easier for me to not drop her. Avery, Mateo and Randy pulled over next to us.

"What happened?" asked Avery.

"She passed out," I said.

"How are we going to get both of them home on bikes?" asked Mateo.

"Let's drop the bikes at Mick's and catch a cab," said Avery.

"Yeah, but how are we getting the bikes there?" asked Mateo.

"I'll ride up there and tell Mick to come and help us," I said. "He's got a car, right?"

"Yeah," said Avery.

"Okay, stay here," I said, gently leaning Ivory against the brick wall.

'But what was this road's name again?'

"The road is Cedar Way," said Avery.

I nodded and rode all the way to Mick's shop, motivated though my legs were burning. I burst in through the back door.

"Mick!" I yelled.

He was organising the World Music section. "Oh hey, li'l girl dude, what's up?"

"Julianna and Ivory passed out and we need help."

His smile evaporated. "Get in the car."

I told him the street name and we drove. When we got there, Julianna and Ivory were resting against the walls of the old building while Mateo and Avery sat next to them. Randy, of course, was examining his bike like it was the most interesting thing in the world.

"Hop in l'il dudes!" said Mick.

"What about the bikes?" asked Avery.

"Do you care about the bike or your sister?"

"My sister, obviously,"

"Good."

I got out and helped them drag Julianna and Ivory to the car.

"Don't worry li'l dude. Claire's on her way to get the bikes with her friends. They'll keep them in the shop and you can pick them up tomorrow," said Mick.

We all squashed in the back of the car, exhausted. Except Randy. He rode home because he didn't want to leave his bike on the street for five minutes.

My legs felt as hard as rocks from how fast I rode to Mick's.

"So where are we going first?" asked Mick.

"Ivory's house," I said.

I looked at Avery. "Get her bandages as soon as you get home."

He nodded.

"Julianna's house is next, her parents are doctors," I said.

"I'm fine to go last," said Mateo. "My parents don't care."

"Okay, then I'll go home after Julianna."

We all got dropped off one by one.

Chapter 28

Julianna: Sisters

I woke up on the couch, bandages all over me. Kaelin was sitting on the edge of the couch. I sat up slowly.

"Jules," she said, "What were you thinking?"

"I'm sorry," I said, "But Ivory went missing!"

"You just got discharged from the hospital and five hours later you were about to go in again!"

I sighed.

"But," she said, "I get it. If my best friend went missing I would go no matter what."

I gave her a small smile. She actually understood how I felt.

"We just need to get past Kai, Lyra, Jaxon and Mum and Dad. They would all flip out," she said.

We laughed softly.

"Juli? Kay?" came a small voice from the hallway.

Our heads snapped around. Lyra. She was standing in the hallway in her purple pyjamas with her turtle plushie.

"Lye, you should be sleeping," said Kaelin.

Lyra ignored her. "Juli, what happened? Did you get hurt again?"

"I'm fine, Lye Lye," I said.

She hugged me with her small arms. "Don't get hurt again. Promise me you won't get hurt."

I felt tears. She was adorable. I hugged her back and kissed her head. "I won't. I promise."

"Promise it to Bubbles too."

I looked down at her turtle plushie. "I promise I won't get hurt, Bubbles."

She smiled.

"Okay Lye, you need to go back bed before Jaxon, Kai and Mum and Dad wake up."

"Okay," she said, rubbing her eyes. She tiptoed up the stairs.

Kaelin stuck her hand out.

"Come on Jules."

She helped me upstairs and to our shared bedroom. I had the bottom bunk and she had the top, so it was easier for me to get in.

"Goodnight Jules," she said.

"Goodnight Kay."

Chapter 29

Ivory: Scars

I woke up the next morning in my bed. I sat up and flinched. I looked down and all the cuts and bruises from the alley were still there. Of course they were, but they were bandaged. Not properly, but like someone had tried their best to help. I wobbled up and went to the bathroom. The scars looked even worse in the light. Dry blood made my shirt cling to my skin. I stumbled out of the bathroom just as Avery came out of his room.

"Ive, you're awake."

"Yeah."

"What happened in the alley?"

I sighed. "You're gonna want to sit down."

We sat in my room. I told him everything. About Blaire, Geniessa, the knife, how I fell. His face went dark, like he would kill.

"When we get back to school..." he said, "bring them to me."

I gulped and nodded.

The door slammed, meaning Mum had left for work.

"Should I call Julianna?" asked Avery. "She really wanted to see you."

I nodded. "But how did you guys find me?"

"We looked everywhere and when we went to Mick's shop he told us you went to the back alley and we found you."

My eyes went wide. They all went out at night to look for me.

"Let's call Julianna," I said.

We dialled her number.

"Hello?" said Julianna.

"Hey, Jules," I said.

"Ive! You're okay!"

"Yeah, wanna come over?"

"Of course."

I hung up.

"I'll call Mateo and once I'm done you can call Addison," said Avery.

He called Mateo and I called Addison. None of them went to school today.

Knock-knock.

We opened the door and the three of them were there. Julianna hugged me straightaway, but gently. Like she knew that my cuts and bruises still hurt.

"How are you, Ive?" asked Julianna.

"I'm actually good," I said.

Addison came and hugged me. "We were so worried about you."

"Guys, come inside," said Avery.

We all sat on the couch and played Boxing. Two people played at a time and the winner stayed in while the loser passed the controller to the next person.

"Duck! Duck! He's gonna swing!" yelled Julianna.

"Thanks Jules!" said Mateo.

"Why did you warn him!? Dammit!" said Avery.

"Avery! Power punch! Power punch! POWER PUNCH!" I yelled.

"Damn. Avery, you got clocked so hard the Atari froze," said Addison.

Avery threw the controller on the floor. "Dammit!"

"Looks like I won," said Mateo.

"My turn!" said Julianna, already grabbing the controller from the floor.

They started playing

"You're landing nothing! Aim, dude!" exclaimed Avery.

"I am!" yelled Mateo.

"Jules! Beat his ass!" I yelled.

"Yeah!" yelled Avery.

"Bro, you're supposed to be on my side!" exclaimed Mateo.

"Jules! Throw a combo!" yelled Addison.

"I won!" exclaimed Julianna, jumping up from the couch and almost knocking over a soda can.

"Hey, you went easy on her!" yelled Avery.

"No, I didn't," said Mateo, smirking.

Julianna didn't notice and kept celebrating her victory.

"It doesn't matter," I said, "but it's my turn!"

We played round after round, not realising what time it was. Then the doorknob rattled.

"What time is it?" asked Avery.

Mateo looked at his watch "7:53."

"Shit, that's when Mum gets home!" Avery whispered harshly. The doorknob rattled louder.

"Hide!" I hissed.

"Where?" asked Julianna.

Mateo tripped over the controller cord. "Shit!"

Julianna's leg bumped into the side of the coffee table and the soda fell and splashed on the carpet. "Oww," she hissed.

Addison desperately tried to turn the Atari off. My eye landed on the blanket on the couch.

"Everyone under the blanket. Now!"

I dove under first, then Avery, then Addison, then Mateo and then Julianna.

"Oww your elbow is in my ribs!" I bit out in a whisper.

"Someone's on my hair!" snapped Julianna in a low voice.

"Sorry," whispered Mateo.

The door flung open and hit the wall with a bang.

"Where are your friends!?" snapped my mum.

I gulped.

"There are three bikes outside and three pairs of shoes. I'm not stupid," said Mum.

The curtain opened quickly, the metal screeching against the wall. She ripped off the blanket and saw all five of us acting as Tetris pieces.

"Hi Mrs Pearce," said Julianna weakly as she waved.

"Everybody out!" my mum shrieked.

Addison, Mateo and Julianna bolted out. I heard a thud outside, like someone had fallen.

'I really hope that wasn't Jules.'

"You two. Kitchen. Now," said my mum in a low voice.

Avery and I gulped in sync.

We sat at the kitchen counter, waiting for whatever punishment she would give us. Mum paced around the kitchen, trying not to explode. I stared at the counter, hoping it would make everything better.

"Do either of you listen to me? Ever?" she asked angrily, like she would kill us.

We stayed silent. It was safer than trying to tell her the truth.

"Avery, you're the older one, why did you let this happen!?" she yelled.

"Mum, it wasn't his fault. It was mine," I said.

"Did I ask you to talk?" she snapped.

I swallowed hard and stayed silent.

"I said no friends. Ever. Do I need to carve it onto your foreheads for you to remember?"

"I said they could come," I said quickly.

Her head snapped towards me. "Do you think you make the rules around here?"

I shook my head.

"Mum, please, it was my fault not hers," said Avery.

"I know it was!" yelled my mum.

"Stop yelling at him!" I snapped.

Avery looked at me wide-eyed, shaking his head and mouthing "Don't."

"What did you say?" asked my mum.

"He didn't do anything wrong."

"Sit. Down." said my mum.

"Make me," I whispered.

She stepped forward. I stood up straight, not flinching even though every part of me was screaming to run.

"I'm not dealing with this right now," she muttered "Ivory Pearce you are grounded for the next two months."

"Fine," I said.

She walked upstairs. I exhaled. I thought the punishment would be way worse.

"Thanks," said Avery.

"No problem."

I went upstairs to my room. I honestly didn't care if I was grounded. I would sneak out anyway.

Chapter 30

Julianna: Broken Promise

We bolted out of Ivory's house. Her mum is like the scariest final boss in a horror game. We were terrified. We ran so fast that the porch light didn't even turn on. We couldn't see where we were going and Mateo tripped on the stairs, I tripped over his leg and Addison tripped over my leg and we all landed on the front pathway with a thud.

"Oww," we all whispered.

"Come on, we need to get out of here," hissed Addison.

We scrambled to our feet and jumped on our bikes.

"Bye," I said.

They said bye and we all went in different directions.

My parents and Kaelin weren't home yet, so I had to sneak past Kai. He was too busy playing video games to notice. I had to climb up the tree on the side of my house to get to my window. My leg burned as soon as it touched the tree. I winced and stumbled back. There was a giant open cut where I fell.

"Great," I muttered.

I climbed up anyway, grimacing every couple of seconds. I finally got into my room. Lyra was there, with Bubbles. She looked me up and down.

"You broke your promise."

"What?"

"You got hurt."

I looked down at my leg and then back at her. "Lyra I'm sorry."

"You promised me you wouldn't get hurt. You promised Bubbles you wouldn't get hurt. You broke your promise to two people." There were tears in her eyes.

"Lye Lye," I said, "I'm sorry."

She went to her room. I felt bad, but there was no way Julianna Kim would last a day without getting hurt. We all know that. I lay on my bed, looking up at the ceiling. I stuck little glow-in-the-dark blue jellyfish stickers up there when I was little. They usually made everything better, but nothing could fix what I'd done this time. I messed up badly. I clutched my bracelet and just started breathing. In and out. I hoped I would eventually fall asleep. I didn't. When I couldn't bear it anymore, I left my room and tiptoed to Lyra's. I opened the door.

"Lye Lye?"

She was sitting on her bed, clutching Bubbles to her chest. She didn't look at me when I walked in.

Translation: She's really mad at me.

I sighed and sat next to her.

"Lye Lye, I'm sorry."

"You broke your promise."

"I know, I probably shouldn't even have made the promise if I wasn't going to keep it."

"Why do you always get hurt?"

I sighed. "There's a few reasons. One, I'm clumsy. Two, because of my fainting and three, because I need to take medicine and I don't like taking it."

"Why do you need medicine?"

"So I don't faint. The doctors gave it to me yesterday." She hugged me. "I forgive you."

I hugged her back. In that moment, her tiny arms hugging my waist and my chin on her head, that perfect moment, I thought,

'If I had her and my friends, nothing in my life could ever ever be bad.'

After I let go of her I had to go back to bed, but I couldn't. Something just felt off. I lay in my bed wide awake for the rest of the night.

Chapter 31

Addison: Sleepless Night

Once I got home, I climbed through the broken window.

'How did Mum still not notice?'

I went to my room and just lay on my bed. I didn't sleep, I didn't have any deep thoughts, just lay there. My gut told me there was something wrong. I told myself everything was fine. It always was, but ever since that visit to the warehouse, something's been off. I didn't sleep. I couldn't.

I watched as the sun rose. I got ready for school. I didn't see my friends until I got there. They looked like they hadn't slept either.

"What happened?" I asked, rubbing my eyes.

Now I felt tired. Not when I wanted to fall asleep, but when school started.

Julianna yawned. "I just couldn't sleep."

Mateo cracked his neck. "Same."

"Me too," said Randy.

"Same here," said Ivory.

CRASH!

We all turned to see Blake standing in front of a broken soccer goal. He stared at it in shock.

"I need some water," said Randy, "but my locker's on the other side of the school. I wish I could have it now."

Suddenly a metal water bottle slammed right at his face and banged into his nose.

"Oww, who threw that?" asked Randy.

We shrugged as the bell rang and we went to our class. Once we got to the Science lab Mrs Emily, our Science teacher, said something that gives every student anxiety.

"Class, I will be putting you in pairs," said Mrs Emily.

I looked around and everyone seemed worried.

"Group one: Bella and Rebecca."

"Yes!" exclaimed Bella and Rebecca in unison.

"Group two: Andy and Anthony."

They looked happy to be together. Suddenly I heard Blaire whispering, not to her minions but to herself.

"Please if you really work make me and Tina together," whispered Blaire.

"Group three: Blaire and Tina."

"Thank you," whispered Blaire.

"Group four: Addison and Ivory."

"Yes!" I whispered.

"Group five: Randy and Blake."

They looked at each other, annoyed.

"Group six: Julianna and Mateo."

They both smiled.

"Group seven: Elizabeth and Omar."

They both gave each other dirty looks.

"Okay class, you will be putting different substances together to make a mixture," said Mrs Emily. "The substances are in front of you. Get mixing!"

Chapter 32

Ivory: Something's Wrong

I couldn't sleep, so I thought of things I could do instead. As I went to turn on my table lamp, my fingers brushed against Saphy. I swore I saw her grow. I measured her every day. Her height was seventy centimetres. I trimmed her almost every day. Otherwise, she would be like one hundred feet. I grabbed the measuring tape from my drawer. I measured her and she was now one metre tall. Something's definitely off. Then I heard banging from Avery's room. He was screaming. I got up and quietly knocked on his door. He opened it, his hair a mess.

"What happened?" I asked.

"My head's just hurting."

"Are you sure? You've been screaming."

He sighed. "I can hear voices. Lots of them. All at once. Even when no one's talking."

"What!?"

"I think I'm losing my mind."

"Just try to sleep," I said. "Hopefully it'll be better by tomorrow."

He massaged his temples. "Hopefully."

I went back to my room and looked up at the ceiling until sunrise. I got ready for school and that's when I actually felt tired.

'Let's just make it through today.'

I went down the stairs and didn't see Avery. I knocked on his door.

He opened it. "Ive... I'm not feeling too good."

"Okay," I said, "get better soon."

I got to school, and everyone was there except Addison. Everyone looked tired, but nothing could get my mind off everything weird that had happened lately, and it was all plant related.

Mateo looked around, confused. "Where's Avery?"

"I think he's losing his mind," I said calmly. I honestly just wanted to see how everyone would react.

"What!?"

"That's what he said."

"I think he means that he's having a headache, Ive," said Julianna.

"But he was screaming in the middle of the night, saying he could hear voices," I said.

"That doesn't sound good," said Randy, who wasn't even paying attention.

Addison walked over, rubbing her eyes. "What happened?"

"I just couldn't sleep," yawned Julianna.

"Same," said Mateo as he cracked his neck loudly.

"Me too," said Randy, playing with his cube.

"Same here," I said.

"CRASH!"

We turned to see Blake standing in front of a broken soccer goal. He stared at it in shock. Something told me weird things were happening to him too and I thought about it. Really thought about it. Avery felt like he was losing his mind, my plants had gone insane, and Blake broke the soccer goal. The common factor. I mean, the only places us three have been together at the same time was the party and the warehouse, and all of the weird things happened right after the warehouse.

"I need some water," said Randy, "but my locker's on the other side of the school. I wish I could have it now."

Suddenly a metal water bottle slammed right at his face and banged into his nose.

"Oww, who threw that?" asked Randy.

The bell rang and we all went to the Science lab. Mrs Emily put us in pairs, and luckily Addison and I were together. We had to make a mixture, so Addison and I mixed salt and water to make a solution. It was the easiest one. Randy and Blake mixed oil and water to make a heterogeneous mixture. We all sat close to each other so that when we finished, we could chat. That's when we heard Mateo raging.

"Bro how do you mix this, it's not mixing!" yelled Mateo.

"Mateo, calm down," said Julianna.

"How the hell is this supposed to work!?" yelled Mateo as he slammed his hand on the table. A flame appeared where his hand had hit the table. It was small at first, a spark. Everyone was fascinated, but it grew fast. Kids screamed and cursed as they ran outside. The smell of smoke filled the air. It was suffocating.

"Holy shit!" shouted Randy, dropping his Rubik's Cube.

The entire class, including Mrs Emily, was already outside, watching and screaming. Julianna was still sitting on her chair and she didn't move. She was a bit *too* calm.

"Julianna! Get up!" I shouted, almost in tears.

"Jules, run!" yelled Mateo, panic cracking in his voice.

Her face went pale, then something changed. Slowly, like she was making a decision she didn't understand herself. We all screamed to get her to run. Then suddenly she did the thing we all feared. She reached out and touched the fire with her bare palm.

But to our surprise the fire disappeared. We stared at her in shock. She calmly looked at us and then at her palm.

"Guys... I think I have powers," whispered Julianna.

Randy coughed nervously. "Or maybe the oxygen just... you know, suffocated the fire when you touched it."

"Maybe."

Julianna finally got up and went outside with us.

"Guys, maybe *I* have powers," said Mateo.

"You probably don't, there is no such thing as having powers," said Randy.

"Then where did the fire come from?" asked Julianna,

"Maybe it was the friction," said Randy.

"Well, then how did your water bottle fly to you, Randy?" asked Julianna.

"Someone could have thrown it at me," said Randy.

"Yeah, I don't think Julianna can just touch fire with her bare hands and put it out," I said.

"And whenever I wanted my mum to do anything for me, she did it without me asking," said Addison.

"Something's wrong," said Mateo

I corrected him. "Very wrong."

We walked to the cafeteria together and sat down to talk about every single weird thing that had happened.

Addison sighed. "Anything weird, powers or not, just say it."

"Only the fire that happened just then for me," said Mateo.

"The other day," Julianna said quietly, "I went to brush my teeth... and more water than my tap could even hold came out."

Addison swallowed hard. "Maybe you have water powers if powers are real."

I nodded. "And Mateo might have fire powers."

Randy looked around cautiously before whispering, "Anything I want floats to me now and my cube moves when I imagine it moving."

"Telekinesis?" I said.

Randy nodded before finally saying, "Maybe."

"My plants grew really quickly when I touched them, and do you guys remember that plant at the hospital? How it grew?" I said.

"Maybe you can control plants," said Addison.

"Maybe Avery is a mind-reader because he can hear voices," said Mateo.

"Let me test something," said Addison cautiously.

Chapter 33

Addison: The Team

In my mind I said,

'Blaire run, stand up and dance on the middle table.'

Across the cafeteria, Blaire suddenly jumped up from her seat, knocking her chair backwards with a loud thud. She bolted to the middle of the cafeteria, jumped onto the table and broke into the worst dance moves I had ever seen. I let out a laugh, half shock, half actual laughter. "I have mind control!"

Julianna laughed and pointed at Blaire. "Now that's something you don't see every day."

We all cracked up, trying not to choke on our food.

"My turn," said Julianna.

She closed her eyes and concentrated. Then she waved her hands and pointed down at her glass. Water shot out from her index finger and her glass was full.

Ivory's eyes went wide and smiled. "Neat!"

Randy shot up excitedly. "Me next!"

He concentrated even harder and a lunch tray with tater tots came floating towards him and landed on our table.

"Anyone hungry?" he asked.

We demolished the tater tots in seconds.

"Can I try?" asked Ivory.

"A tot or your powers?" Mateo teased.

We all started laughing.

"My powers," said Ivory, still laughing.

She got up and moved towards a tree. We all watched her from inside and as soon as she touched the tree it grew a couple of metres taller.

We were all shocked. She came back inside, smiling.

"Wow, I actually have powers!" she exclaimed.

"My turn," said Mateo.

"Be careful," said Randy.

"It's fine, if it gets out of control I'll put it out," said Julianna.

Mateo waved his hands and concentrated harder than any of us had. He accidentally threw a small fireball at someone's lunch tray, which fell on the carpeted floor in the hallway, setting the carpet on fire.

"Oh no," said Randy.

The fire spread rapidly across the school.

"Quick, you guys get out of here I'll stop the fire," said Julianna, already trying to get us out.

"It's too dangerous," said Mateo.

"Yeah, what if you can't get out?" said Ivory.

"No one stays alone," I said.

"We'll help you," said Ivory.

"I don't think Mateo will be much help, but I'll help," said Randy.

The sprinklers above us made a weird creaking noise, then suddenly water burst out, but it wasn't the system. It was Julianna, hands raised, pulling water from the air. The problem? Some of the water splashed across the floor, racing toward the electrical sockets. The lights flickered.

And then everything went black.

The water had taken the lights out. It was only a matter of time before things got out of hand.

"Julianna, try to put out as much as you can," I said.

"Got it," said Julianna as she ran toward the burning hallway.

"Randy, use your telekinesis to grab as many fire extinguishers as you can and use them," I said.

"Okay!" Randy bolted down the corridor, eyes darting everywhere until a dozen red fire extinguishers began sliding and clattering toward him like metal soldiers answering his call.

"Ivory, go outside and grow some plants to get people out of the building," I said.

"On it," said Ivory, running outside.

"Mateo, try and see if you can manipulate the fire and try to put it out if you can," I said.

"Alright," said Mateo.

I stayed back, trying to use my mind control to get the firefighters here, but for some reason it wasn't working. I began to worry that maybe I didn't have powers anymore. Then I realised every time I had used my powers it had been more than one hour apart. I had to wait to recharge. Instead of wasting time, I called the fire department.

The air grew hotter and thicker. I started choking on the smoke. All I could see was a thick black cloud of smoke but then, suddenly, the blaze began shrinking. Flames curled back on themselves, sparks dying midair. Mateo stood in the smoke, his arms shaking, sweat pouring down his face. Beside him, Julianna pressed her palms outwards, water shooting from her hands, dousing the worst of it. She was struggling, I could hear her ragged breathing from almost the other side of the cafeteria. Behind them, extinguishers floated through the air like ghosts, spraying on their own. Randy's doing.

The fire went quiet. The building breathed again. And so did we. Outside, we all ran to the grass and collapsed. My lungs burned, but laughter bubbled up anyway. Half hysteria, half relief.

"I can't wait to tell Avery about what he missed today!" exclaimed Ivory.

Mateo smiled. "Yeah, he missed out on a lot."

Julianna sat up. "Was he lucky or unlucky?"

I sat up too. "Unlucky."

"But we almost died!" yelled Randy.

I looked at each of them. "But today was the day we became a team."

Randy raised an eyebrow. "Weren't we already a team?"

Ivory nodded. "Yeah, a boring History project team."

I smiled. "But now we're a super team with powers and we just completed our first mission."

We all went back to Ivory's house to hang out and to see Avery. He came downstairs in his pyjamas, rubbing his temples.

"How you feeling, Avery?" asked Mateo.

"Yeah, Avery, how are you?" asked Randy.

"I'm fine. Just a headache," Avery muttered.

"No, you have powers like we all do," I said.

"What?"

Ivory tapped his shoulder "Avery, watch."

She touched a plant and it grew two metres in the blink of an eye.

"What the hell!"

"We think you might be a mind reader," I said.

"Who wants to be my test subject?" said Avery.

All of us backed away.

"Fine, I'll do it," said Ivory.

Avery concentrated and then his expression changed; he looked like he had seen a ghost.

"Ivory you…"

Ivory cut him off. "Shut up!"

The rest of us burst out laughing.

"Guys, we need cool code names!" exclaimed Julianna. "I want to be Oceria!"

"Call me Sorren!" declared Mateo.

"Levark," Randy said simply.

"I'll be Nyxia," I announced.

"I'm Seraphyll!" said Ivory proudly.

"Cerephiel" Avery added smoothly.

Ivory looked confused. "That's literally what I just said."

"I'll change the spelling," said Avery.

"Come up with a different name!" yelled Ivory.

"If you make me change my name I'll tell everyone why you told me to shut up," said Avery, smirking.

"Fine, keep the damn name," said Ivory, clearly pissed off.

We were all laughing until...

Click.

The doorknob rattled.

We shut up and froze.

"Quick, do you guys remember what happened yesterday!?" whispered Avery harshly.

"What?" asked Randy.

"Doesn't matter, but we need to go!" hissed Ivory.

The doorknob rattled again, sharper this time. We froze. My heart thumped so loud I swore everyone could hear it. As we ran up the stairs, Mateo's sneaker bounced down the stairs behind him, the squeak echoing like a gunshot. He cursed under his breath, hopping awkwardly up one foot before Avery yanked him into his room and slammed the door.

Ivory didn't waste a second. She gripped my wrist and Julianna's, dragging us towards her room. We ran until Julianna tripped over Mateo's abandoned shoe, I tripped over Julianna, and we nearly went down hard, until Ivory grabbed us both by the elbows and hauled us upright.

"Come on," she hissed.

We made it to her room and dove under the bed, dust coating my hoodie, Julianna squishing me against the bed legs. Ivory bolted down the stairs.

A few minutes later footsteps creaked up the staircase. Slow. Heavy. Coming closer. I clamped my hand over my mouth, praying she wouldn't hear us breathe.

Chapter 34

Ivory: Hide and Seek

"Avery, Ivory, I'm home," said my mum, slamming the door behind her, angry as always.

"Oh h-hey M-Mum," I said nervously.

"Ivory, why are you stuttering?" she snapped.

"She told me it was a big day of school, and she's really tired now," said Avery. "Come on, sis you should go to bed."

He pushed me up the stairs and into my room.

"You dork, you almost blew it!" Avery rasped in a low voice.

"I'm sorry," I whispered.

"It's fine."

"Guys, I'm a bit suffocated in here," whispered Julianna, who was hiding under my cramped bed with Addison.

"Oww, that was my face!" hissed Addison.

"Sorry," whispered Julianna.

Avery's eyes widened. If Julianna and Addison were making this much noise then Mateo and Randy would be making ten times more. He bolted for his own room just as Mum's footsteps thundered up the stairs. Mum banged on the door. I jumped.

"Oh h-hey mum," I said, opening the door.

She pushed past me aggressively and began sticking her hand under my bed and checking my closet. My heart felt like it was going to come out of my chest.

"W-what are you l-looking for?" I asked anxiously.

"Suspects," she said, not looking at me.

"W-why?" I asked.

She dangled the shoe between two fingers, frowning. "Whose is this? You know I nearly cracked my head open, tripping over it."

My stomach twisted.

'Don't laugh, don't laugh, don't laugh.'

I bit my lip so hard I tasted copper, fighting not to laugh. The thing looked like it belonged to Bigfoot.

"I-i-is that Avery's?" I asked weakly.

Mum froze because of the sudden realisation. She walked over to Avery's room and started shouting, "I almost tripped on this when I was coming upstairs. Don't leave your shoes on the stairs!"

I heard the shoe land with a thud on the wooden floor. I heard her footsteps thundering in the hallway.

"ACHOOO!"

I froze. It came from Avery's room. I bit my fist, every nerve screaming.

'If she checked... if she even peeked...'

But luckily Mum only sighed in irritation.

"Clean this place up," she muttered, before stomping back down the stairs.

I exhaled a shaky breath of relief. Then I whispered to the bedframe, "Okay. Window. Now."

Addison and Julianna wriggled out, their hair and clothes full of dust, eyes wide.

"From the second floor with no bush at the bottom!?" Addison snapped in a whisper.

"With no rope?" Julianna hissed under her breath.

"You'll be fine. Now go before my mum comes back into my room and my dad gets in the driveway," I bit out quietly.

They climbed out of the window, both making it down safely. Outside, Mateo and Randy were also climbing down. Somehow Mateo's sneaker flew out the window after him. Randy must've helped with his powers, as it landed perfectly in his hands. He shoved the shoe on and they bolted for the street, disappearing into the sunset.

I closed the window quietly, wiped the sweat off my palms and sat on the edge of my bed. My heart was still racing.

Avery poked his head in. "That was close."

"Too close," I whispered.

He gave a humourless smile, but I saw the way his hand trembled on the doorframe. "If Mum or Dad ever catch them here again…"

He didn't finish. He didn't have to.

When he left, I lay back and stared at Saphy. I curled onto my side, clutching my pillow tight. For the first time since this all started, a thought crept in that I didn't want to face:

'What if Blaire wasn't the biggest problem anymore?'

Chapter 35

Addison: Gossip and Rumours

"Detention again Addison?" asked my Mum, who was waiting for me at the table as always.

"No, I was at a friend's house."

"Without asking me!?"

"Do I have to ask to go to detention!?"

"No, but that's a school thing. You need to ask before going to your random friend's house!"

"Oh my god Mum, I'm fourteen and I have a life. I'm not a little kid anymore, just stop trying to control me!"

I stormed up to my room. Once again, I didn't come down that night even though I was hungry. It was fine because I was going to have lunch the next day anyway.

Somehow the next two weeks went by like a summer breeze. Every single day after school we practiced our powers near my locker since no one else went there.

It was just a usual Tuesday and we were practicing. Things were normal, calm even. Randy pissed Avery off and they were chasing each other. The rest of us were just using our powers while we laughed at them.

Suddenly Ivory yelped and weeds shot out of the ground. One of them wrapped around Randy's leg while he was running. He tripped face-planted on the ground. Avery was running too fast to stop and he tripped over Randy.

"Sorry," said Ivory.

Avery sat up. "It's all good. Randy broke my fall."

Randy just groaned.

We all burst out laughing.

"Ivory, why'd you even jump in the first place?" asked Julianna.

Ivory laughed. "I thought I saw a cockroach."

That made everyone laugh even more. After about twenty minutes we heard Julianna and Mateo laughing and whispering.

"What are you guys talking about?" asked Ivory.

"Nothing," said Mateo, quickly.

"Seriously, what is it?" asked Avery.

"It's a surprise!" said Julianna.

We looked at them, still suspicious, but we kept practicing our powers anyway.

'It couldn't have been anything bad right?'

After school we went to Galaxy Plaza. We were hungry so we went to the burger joint, Burgerbite. We sat in the booth closest to the window. The red and white neon lights were blinding. We ordered pretty much straightaway and got our food. Mateo took a bite from his burger.

"The burgers here are amazing."

Julianna stole a chip from him. "I know, right?"

"Okay, you know how we have assigned seats in Maths now," said Randy, a bit too excitedly.

"Yeah," I said cautiously.

"Well, I'm sitting next to Elizabeth and Alya and they gossip a lot!" said Randy.

"I'm sitting next to Mark and Orion." said Mateo. "They were arguing about who would win in a fight: a bear or a shark."

All of us burst out laughing.

I spat out my soda. "What!?"

"Yeah, and then Mr Bentley got so sick of it he told them the bear would win and then he went back to teaching."

"Ohh, that's why he went to your table," said Ivory.

"Aww man, I was rooting for the shark," said Julianna.

That made everyone laugh again.

"Man, I've got it way worse," said Avery. "Anthony was giving Omar flirting lessons again."

"What do you mean *again*?" I asked.

Mateo face palmed. "Did he trip over Tina's bag again?"

"Nope, worse. Anthony told him to lean on her desk like he was the main character in a high school movie," said Avery.

"And?" asked Randy.

"He leaned and the table leaned back. They both hit the floor."

"So, Science wasn't the only time he pulled that move?" asked Julianna.

"The guy's resilient," said Mateo.

"More like stupid," I said.

Laughter bubbled up again.

"I heard from Tina and Rebecca that Dylan from the other class 'accidentally' ran into Bella in the hallway for the third time today," said Ivory.

"She keeps ducking into the nearest classroom each time," said Julianna.

"No, but what's even crazier is the gossip I heard," said Randy.

"Spill," said Julianna.

"So apparently, Tina likes Blake and we all know Blaire's obsessed with him, but apparently Anthony likes Blaire and Tina also likes Anthony and Omar likes Tina."

"My brain couldn't process what the hell you said," said Mateo.

"Wait, so Tina likes two guys who are complete opposites?" asked Julianna.

Randy took a sip from his soda. "The girl's crazy."

"What was even crazier was what happened in the bathroom," said Avery.

"Oh my god. I can't with them," said Mateo.

"What happened?" asked Julianna.

"Mark and Orion were fighting about the bear and shark thing again. Someone shoved and the next thing you know, there's paper towels flying and soap everywhere," said Mateo.

"They broke a dispenser," said Avery.

"You saw that?" asked Ivory.

"Nope. Heard it. I was washing my hands. Mark was trying to tag in his friend."

My eyes went wide. "They turned it into a tag team match?"

Mateo nodded. "Full wrestling commentary, too. One of them yelled, 'From the top rope!' before climbing the sink."

"Did anyone stop them?" asked Randy.

Avery leaned back and nodded. "The bell did. They ran like criminals when it rang."

"Okay, I am officially scared of that bathroom," I said.

We laughed again.

"Bella said that they're bringing back uniforms next year," said Julianna.

Mateo groaned "Didn't we just get rid of those?"

"Great, hair tied up, no jewellery and stupid red and grey all over again," muttered Ivory with her arms crossed.

"It's okay, we'll just do what we did last time," said Avery.

"What did you do last time?" I asked, suspicion in my voice.

"We found every way around the dress code."

"Every?"

He nodded.

We kept eating. Randy had this weird look on his face, so I did the only logical thing. I threw a chip at him. It hit his glasses and his head shot up.

"What was that for?"

"What happened?" I asked.

"Nothing."

"Randy, spill."

"Okay, I heard a rumour."

"So? We always hear rumours," said Ivory.

Randy sighed. "It was about two people from our group."

We all looked at each other.

"Who committed a crime?" asked Avery.

Randy adjusted his glasses. "No one."

"Who was it about?" asked Julianna.

"Elizabeth and Alya told everyone that you... a-and Mateo... well... c-confessed that... y-you g-g-guys l-like each other."

Mateo went pink and Julianna choked on her milkshake. The bubbler nearby exploded.

"Jules! Are you okay?" asked Mateo as he started patting her back.

"Oh my god she's dying!" I yelled.

"I'm fine!" she said, still coughing. "Wrong pipe!"

She coughed a few more times before turning to Randy, her face bright pink. "You...What did you just say!?"

"That you and Mateo confessed. Elizabeth said she saw you guys 'acting couple-y' near the lockers."

Mateo almost choked on his chip.

"That's not true!" yelled Julianna.

"We're not...We're not like that!" yelled Mateo.

"Exactly! We're just friends!"

"Right! Totally just... friends!"

They started talking over each other, stumbling over their words. I caught Ivory and Avery exchanging a knowing glance. Like they knew something I didn't.

"Wait, hold up. Who started this?" I asked.

"Elizabeth," said Randy.

"Flashbacks," muttered Avery.

I stopped mid-sip. "So, this isn't new?"

"Nope, fourth grade debut. Still running. Just got a new outfit," said Ivory.

Julianna groaned into her hands, Mateo tried to disappear into his hoodie. The memory haunted both of them.

"Since year four?" I asked.

"Yep, the 'Mateo and Julianna like each other' saga never ended, apparently," said Avery.

Randy shrugged, trying to hide a grin but failing miserably. "Well, it's not exactly unbeliev-"

"Randy!" Ivory snapped, slapping the back of his head.

He put his hands up like they would save him, "Geez, geez I was joking!"

"Sure, you were," muttered Avery.

"She's doing it for attention again. S-s-she always does that," said Julianna, fumbling over her words.

"Yeah, she just... It's nothing. We were just talking about the project. N-not whatever she thinks," Mateo said quickly.

I slammed my soda on the table. "She's lucky I don't go over there and make her swallow her words."

Ivory twirled her straw. "She's by the fountain."

I stood up, almost knocking the table over, and grabbed my bag.

Avery grabbed my wrist. "Addi. No."

I shook his hand off. "Addi. Yes."

I stomped over to the fountain. Ivory caught up to me, clearly pissed, but not surprised. Mateo and Julianna walked behind us while Avery and Randy walked behind them, Randy obviously grabbing extra chips for the road.

Elizabeth and Alya were leaning against the fountain with at least twenty shopping bags. Julianna caught up to me and tugged my sleeve.

"Addi it's fine, just leave it."

"Nope," I said, "she crossed a line."

Mateo sighed. "Can we at least make sure that there aren't any security guards this time?"

I pushed through the crowd and shouted, "Elizabeth!"

She looked at me and grinned.

"Addison, you travel with a circus now?" she said.

"If you've got something to say to them, say it to their faces."

She tilted her head innocently. "About what?"

Randy grinned, still eating chips. "Apparently, Mateo and Julianna's romantic subplot."

I shot him a death glare. Elizabeth smirked.

"Oh, that," she said, "you came all the way here for that story."

"It's not a story, it's a lie," snapped Mateo.

Alya looked at him. "If it's a lie why are you so defensive about it?"

Everyone went silent and people around us started to stare.

"Maybe because you've been spreading the same shit since Year 4," said Ivory. "Doesn't it get old after five years?"

"It's not even a rumour," said Elizabeth.

"Yeah, it's so obvious that they like each other," said Alya.

Julianna came forward and shoved Alya. She stumbled back, knocking half the shopping bags into the fountain.

"My new clothes!" Elizabeth screeched.

Alya shot up and shoved Julianna back. Julianna stumbled but didn't fall. Ivory swung at the side of Alya's head.

Crack.

The sound felt like it echoed through the entire mall. No one made a sound.

Alya touched the side of her head, blood on her fingertips. She stared at them and shrieked. Elizabeth came forward and lunged at Ivory. Avery stepped in before she could do anything. He pushed her; not enough to hurt her, just enough to keep her back.

"You don't touch her," he said, voice scarily calm.

Elizabeth clutched her head. Avery must've been putting things in her head *literally*, but she didn't take the hint and pushed past him. She shoved Ivory into the wall.

The plants around us shot up, each one grabbing a part of Elizabeth. First her wrists, then her ankles and then her face. Ivory controlled the plants to make her come closer.

"You don't ever piss me off," she whispered, before making the plants drop Elizabeth to the ground with a yelp.

Alya ran at Julianna again. Mateo and I were about to step in. Fire glowing from his hands, and me ready to control her mind, but Julianna suddenly shot water out of her palm, sending Alya flying backwards into the fountain.

Randy came over, chips floating behind him with a translucent orange glow. "Wow you sure showed them!"

"Randy, shut up," we all said.

"Come on, we need to cool off," I said.

"Where?" asked Avery.

"The rink!" said Randy.

Before you know it, we're sitting in the locker room of the roller rink putting our skates on.

"How do you lace this?" I yelled, after restarting for the tenth time.

"Calm down," said Avery, whose laces were somehow done perfectly.

"We'll help you," said Ivory.

Both of them helped me lace my skates.

"How did you guys do that?" I asked, staring at them as if they had just performed witchcraft.

"Ten years of practice," said Avery.

"Come on," said Ivory.

We went first, me being a disaster on wheels. Ivory and Avery balanced me. We stepped into the rink. I slipped instantly.

"Got you," said Avery.

"Yeah, just relax and you'll be fine," said Ivory.

"I've never skated before," I mumbled.

"What?" asked Avery.

I sighed and said it louder. "I've never skated before."

"That's okay," said Ivory.

"We'll teach you," said Avery.

Mateo, Julianna and Randy got on the rink.

"Why did it take you so long?" asked Ivory.

"Randy put his skates on the wrong way," said Mateo.

Randy was clutching the rail like his life depended on it. "Shut up."

We all laughed.

Randy pushed off the rail way too fast and immediately lost control.

"AHHH!" he yelled before crashing into a padded wall. He hugged it like it was his best friend.

That made everyone laugh more. Avery grabbed one of my hands while Ivory grabbed the other.

"Okay, so first you slide one leg and then the second one," said Avery.

"Just stand straight while bending your knees and you'll be fine," said Ivory.

I gulped and nodded. I did what they said. I pushed off with my right leg and then the left and then back to the right.

"You're doing it," said Avery.

I smiled. Back in Clearridge we didn't have roller rinks. Just dark, grungy alleyways that we used to hang out in after school.

Then I lost my balance. I wobbled forward and they both steadied me before I could fall.

"We've got you," said Ivory.

I gave a small smile and nodded.

They kept teaching me and I ended up slipping only about four times.

"Okay, on your own now," said Avery.

"What?" I asked

"Yep," said Ivory, "you'll be fine."

I swallowed hard. "Okay."

I T-posed, hoping it would help me keep my balance.

"Addi," said Avery, "just breathe and you'll be fine."

"Yeah," said Ivory.

I took a deep breath and pushed.

'Left foot, right foot, left foot, right foot.'

I stared at my skates and smiled. I was actually doing it. Then a hand grabbed my wrist. I looked up and a huge wall was inches away from my face. I turned to my side. It was Avery grabbing my wrist.

"You almost crashed."

I looked at the wall and then back at him and whispered, "Thanks."

"Come on," he said, "Randy crashed into a little kid and Ivory went to watch the parent's reaction."

We skated back to them, and I was a lot more careful with where I was going.

Chapter 36

Julianna: Total Chaos (on Wheels)

After all that drama with stupid Elizabeth and stupid Alya, we went to the roller rink to calm down.

"How do you lace this!?" Addison yelled.

"Calm down," said Avery.

"We'll help you," said Ivory.

They helped her with her skates while she stared at them as if they had confessed to murder.

"How did you guys do that?" she asked.

"Ten years of practice," said Avery.

"Come on," said Ivory.

The three of them left, leaving Randy, Mateo and me.

Randy being Randy immediately put his left skate on his right foot.

"Wrong foot buddy," said Mateo, who was already tying his first skate.

Randy shot him a death glare. "I knew that."

I snickered and Mateo smirked. "Whatever you say."

I tried to tie my first skate at least five times but failed. Addison was right for going crazy. I huffed, blowing my fringe out of my face.

"You have to be gentle," said Mateo.

I looked up at him, and of course his skates were already tied perfectly.

"This is so frustrating," I said.

"I know, just don't pull them too hard otherwise you'll end up like Randy." He pointed at Randy at the skate rental counter, trying to return the skates with broken laces.

I giggled and that helped me calm down. I exhaled and actually tied my laces properly.

"Thanks," I said.

"No problem."

The three of us wobbled towards the rink.

"Why did it take you so long?" asked Ivory.

"Randy put his skates on the wrong way," said Mateo.

Randy was clutching the rail so tightly his knuckles went white. "Shut up."

We all burst out laughing.

Randy pushed away from the rail too hard, and he built up way too much speed and instantly lost control. He yelled, making everyone in the rink turn towards him before he hugged the padded wall like he would never let go. That made everyone laugh even more.

Addison, Avery and Ivory skated closer to the middle. I stayed near the edge, clutching onto the rail like my life depended on it.

"Come on, it's not that bad," said Mateo.

"I skated once and broke my leg," I said.

"Well, that won't happen this time," he said, "probably."

That got a small laugh out of me.

"Besides, you can just grab onto something if you lose your balance."

"Okay," I said hesitantly.

I let go of the rail and skated.

"How can you skate this good?" asked Mateo.

"Okay, maybe it wasn't the first time when I broke my leg."

I did a spin. I wouldn't get hurt too badly if I fell. Right?

Suddenly Randy zoomed past us. We both almost lost our balance.

"Randy!" yelled Mateo. "Watch where you're going!"

Randy, of course not watching where he was going, crashed into a couple holding hands and all three of them fell.

"Sorry!" he said before skating back to us, way too fast.

He kept doing circles and trying to copy some spin move a girl who was clearly trained did, and he failed miserably. He spun too fast and crashed straight into me. I yelped and crashed straight into Mateo. We all landed in a heap on the floor.

"My bad," said Randy. "Gives me nostalgia from when I hit that couple."

"That was two minutes ago," I said.

"Yeah, it was." He looked really dizzy.

"Come on, let's go," said Mateo, holding both his hands out.

I took one and he helped me up. Randy grabbed the other one, but as soon as he was upright, he went right back down again. Mateo just face-palmed and left him there. We skated away from him just in case he started another disaster.

"This is actually fun," I said.

"Yeah, it is."

"What are the odds that Randy crashes into someone in the next five minutes?"

He laughed. "You're being way too optimistic."

And right on cue Randy crashed into a little six-year-old, knocking her fairy floss onto the floor. We both bit back a laugh.

"Let's go," he said, still stifling his laugh.

We skated up to Avery and Addison and all four of us burst out laughing.

"The poor kid," said Addison, wiping a tear from her eye.

"That kid wasn't warned that Randy would be on skates tonight," said Avery.

"Whose idea was it to even let him on skates?" I asked.

"His own," said Mateo.

That started another round of laughter. Randy and Ivory skated up to us.

"Great, I'm down twenty bucks," said Randy.

"You deserved it," said Addison.

"Come on, let's race!" said Ivory.

We lined up horizontally.

"Okay, first person back here wins," said Ivory.

"Three, two, one, go!" yelled Avery.

Addison looked like she was running rather than skating, and she tripped straight away. Avery and Ivory caught her arms before she face-planted. Randy was tripping over everything that could be tripped over and bumping into everything that could be bumped into. Mateo swerved and stumbled over his own foot. I grabbed his sleeve before he fell.

"You good?"

"Yeah," he said.

We both started skating faster, even though we probably weren't catching up to Ivory, who was doing Michael Jackson's Moonwalk on skates. "See ya, suckers."

Avery skated after her and actually caught up, but instead of going past her to win, he dragged her away from the group of kids that she had almost fallen onto. Addison was behind us, and she came with so much speed she couldn't stop and hit both of us.

"That's twice now," said Mateo.

We all stayed on the floor and giggled. We couldn't get up, so this was better. After Avery and Ivory crossed the finish line together, we clapped and stood up.

The lights changed to a calm blue and purple and 'Time After Time' by Cyndi Lauper played. Everyone was going slowly. Our group joined in and all of us went slowly and peacefully.

"This is the best way to end the day," I said.

"Yeah," said Mateo.

"Definitely," said Ivory.

We skated around the rink together, smiling and laughing, until Randy decided he wanted to copy some couple's spin move on his own. He tried it and crashed straight into Addison, who grabbed Avery so she wouldn't fall, who instinctively grabbed Ivory, who just accepted her fate.

Mateo and I laughed and then helped them up.

"You guys, okay?" he asked.

"Never better," said Avery.

We helped them all up and not even five seconds later, Randy lost control of his skates and bumped into Addison, who bumped into Avery, who bumped into Ivory, who bumped into me, and I bumped into Mateo, and we all went down like dominos.

"Randy!" we all yelled.

Then Cyndi Lauper's 'Girls Just Want to Have Fun' played.

"Round two!" yelled Addison as she skated to the middle and tried to spin. Surprisingly, she actually did it.

"Be careful!" Avery called out.

Addison ignored him and attempted another spin, which didn't go too well. She tripped over her own foot and went down hard with a loud thud. We immediately skated over to her.

"Are you okay?" asked Ivory as she extended her hand to Addison.

Addison took it and laughed. "Yep. Just the world's way of telling me I probably shouldn't try spins yet."

"With a bit of practice, you'll do it in no time," said Avery.

Addison smiled.

Randy skated towards us, carefully this time. With a giant bucket of popcorn.

Mateo sighed, definitely done with Randy's stupidity. "Why?"

"Snacks on skates," he said.

"Randy, you're going to get us kicked out," I said.

"Relax."

He threw a piece of popcorn at Avery's head. It landed in his hair.

Avery picked it out and threw it on the ground. "Really?"

Randy skated around with the bucket, holding it like it was gold.

Addison chased after him, clearly forgetting what happens when she isn't careful.

"I want some!" she yelled.

Avery sighed and went after both of them, either to make sure Addison didn't fall again or for the popcorn, maybe both.

"Come on," I said, already pulling Mateo to the chaos of our group. "We're here to have fun!"

He rolled his eyes and smiled. "Whoever doesn't get the popcorn pays for dinner!"

I nodded and we both bolted, and the rest of our group heard the deal too.

"Team?" Mateo whispered.

I didn't say anything.

We all chased Randy like he owed us his entire house. He screamed and tried to skate as fast as he could. Addison, clearly determined, jumped on his back. Randy cried out in surprise and face-planted on the floor. Addison was still on his back. She grabbed the popcorn and yelled, "I'm not paying!"

She scrambled up and skated away. The rest of us chased her, leaving Randy on the floor.

He groaned, "Help me."

Ivory moonwalked again and smoothly snatched the popcorn from Addison's hands. "Mine now," she said, taking a piece and popping it into her mouth.

I skated from behind her and grabbed the popcorn bucket.

Avery skated towards me.

"Mateo! Heads up!" I yelled.

I chucked the popcorn bucket at him; popcorn flying across the rink as it fell. Mateo skated towards it and jumped, actually jumped, and grabbed it mid-air, before landing on the ground and skating while eating like he didn't just pull a ninja move. We all just stared at him, jaws dropped.

"Ave man!" Mateo called out, tossing a piece of popcorn in his mouth. "You're paying for dinner!"

Avery sighed.

The manager of the rink came up to us.

"You guys have broken four violations in your half an hour here."

"What did we do?" I asked.

"First, you guys didn't wear any protection."

"Seriously?" said Avery, gliding over.

"Second, there is a strict no racing policy."

Addison skated over. "Then what's the point of a roller rink?"

The manager ignored her. "Third you brought food onto the rink."

We all looked at Randy, who was still lying on the floor.

"And finally, you need adult supervision if you are under the age of sixteen."

"Hang on," said Mateo.

"What?" asked the manager, clearly frustrated.

Mateo pulled out his fake ID. "I'm eighteen."

The manager looked from Mateo to his ID, not convinced that a fourteen-year-old boy was actually eighteen, but he couldn't say anything about it, so he just huffed and muttered, "Well you still broke three violations," before going back to his office.

We went to the locker room and took our skates off

"Well, you saved us from one violation," said Avery.

"You're welcome," said Mateo.

"And Ave, now you're paying for dinner," said Addison.

"I know," he said.

They got up and returned their skates.

"Thanks for the popcorn," Mateo said.

I smiled. "No problem."

We went back to Burgerbite for dinner on Avery and then we all went home, waiting for what tomorrow would bring.

Chapter 37

Addison: Operation R.A.D.

The next day was just a random Wednesday, or so I thought. I was about to go to school when I heard a knock at the door. I answered it. There stood a man dressed in a black suit. He looked like an important person. Like he was coming to collect taxes or something.

"Hello," I said.

"Hi, are you Addison Taylor Moore?" he asked with a smile. His smile was too wide for his face.

"Yes, I am," I replied cautiously.

"Come with us, you have won an award for your school!"

I went with him into a black van where I saw Ivory, Avery, Mateo, Julianna and Randy. I smiled at them, and they smiled back, but they looked stiff. Like something was wrong.

"Kids, there are a few more students we have to pick up," said the man. "Just sit tight."

The car ride was bumpy, and everyone was weirdly quiet. Julianna kept rubbing her bracelet as if it could teleport us out of here, Mateo sat next to her, just looking around quickly, while Ivory kept fiddling with her necklace. Avery was next to her, making sure she was okay. Randy of course just played with his Rubik's Cube like he couldn't care less that we were in stranger's black van. I understood why they felt weird. Being in this van just felt *wrong*.

The car stopped abruptly at Blake's house. He got into the van and for once he wasn't using his Game & Watch, but he looked sad and exhausted, with huge bags under his eyes. The silence was killing me, but everyone looked like they were so uncomfortable that they couldn't breathe.

"This is the last person to pick up," said the man.

We pulled up in front of a small old house that hadn't been painted in years, with a front yard hadn't been trimmed in ages. It smelled gross.

Avery scrunched his nose. "Who lives here?"

"Miss Belinda Claire Genevieve Pembroke," said the man.

We were all confused. Pembroke was Blaire's last name, but her first name was Blaire, not Belinda, and her parents were rich, so she wouldn't live there.

Surprisingly, Blaire got into the van and gave us a dirty look.

"Just so you know, I was at my poor cousin's house for a sleepover."

We all ignored her, which made her talk more. "So I won a beauty award. What did these guys win?"

"No, Blaire you won the clueless bimbo award because that's what you are," said Ivory.

"Shut up, spaz!"

"Quiet down in there!" yelled the driver.

We pulled over at a business building. It was neat and perfect. A little bit too neat and perfect. Not a single pen was out of place.

They took us to a room that looked like an interrogation room.

"Kids, have you been to that old roller-skate factory downtown?" asked the man.

"What's a 'rolly' skate?" asked Blaire.

"Ignore her sir, she's just stupid," said Randy.

"Yes, I can see that," said the man. "Anyway, we think some radiation might have gotten in your bodies."

"What kind of radiation?" asked Avery.

"The mutating kind," said the man.

"Excuse me, who are you?" asked Mateo.

He stood up menacingly.

"I am Mr Blackwood. Now if you don't do as I say I'll end you all!"

We were all scared.

"Lock them up," said Mr Blackwood.

"What!?" Avery barked.

"I don't know who you think you are, but no one tries to kidnap me and my friends," said Mateo.

He was about to hit him, but Mr Blackwood's cane swung fast. Mateo collapsed before we could blink, blood on his temple. Julianna shrieked. Avery lunged forward, but Ivory yanked him back, terror in her eyes.

"Lock these kids up," barked Mr Blackwood.

His men came and threw us into a cramped cell.

Randy looked at Mateo, who was on the ground.

"He needs medical attention."

"Addison use your powers to get us out of here," said Julianna, panic cracking her voice.

"No. Addison needs to save her powers for when we need it most," snapped Randy.

Julianna started tearing up. "We need a doctor!"

"How is her power going to help that!"

Everyone went quiet. That's when we heard a groan.

"I think he's waking up!" exclaimed Avery.

"Where are we?" slurred Mateo.

"We're trapped," I said.

"How are we going to get out?"

"That's what we're trying to figure out, but Julianna keeps crying for no reason," said Randy.

Julianna sat down, clutched her knees, and started crying.

"See!" exclaimed Randy.

"I'm-m s-scared," said Julianna between sobs.

Ivory bent down next to Julianna and hugged her.

"It's okay, we're all scared," said Ivory.

"Yeah, we just need to find a way out of here," said Avery.

"Any thoughts?" I asked.

"Maybe Randy should stop yelling at scared girls," said Mateo.

"Yeah Randy," said Ivory.

Randy rolled his eyes.

"Where is my trophy?" demanded Blaire.

"You idiot, there is no trophy!" yelled Blake.

"Blake, I think you have super strength because of how you broke the goal," said Avery.

He sighed. "Yeah, I do. I broke my Game & Watch as well."

"Can you get us out of here?" I asked.

"I'll try."

He tried to bend the bars, but nothing happened.

"Weird. It's like you lost your powers," said Mateo.

"Mateo, try to burn the bars," said Julianna.

"My powers! They're gone!"

"So, you finally noticed?" asked Mr Blackwood.

"Why are you doing this to us?" I asked.

"Since you will not be able to get out, I'll tell you."

We were all nervous.

"I will release the same radiation that mutated you guys, only at a higher dose, which will kill everyone who breathes it in, except people who already mutated like you guys," said Mr Blackwood.

"How did you know that we would mutate?" asked Mateo.

"I planted the substance and now I would like you to meet Mrs Blackwood," said Mr Blackwood.

Suddenly a figure emerged from the shadows.

Mrs Lindsey.

We all gasped.

"I knew at least one group would choose roller-skating," she sneered. "Predictable pawns."

She shot Blaire a look. "Though I wish you weren't in it."

"So, everyone, including our parents, will die?" asked Julianna, her voice shaking.

"Yes," said Mr Blackwood.

"But why?" asked Ivory.

"So that I can rule this country and take over more countries and finally rule the world. Then I'll find survivors, and they will repopulate so that there are still working people and working facilities," said Mr Blackwood.

"Where is my trophy!?" yelled Blaire.

"You idiot, I just explained that I kidnapped you and there is no trophy!" shouted Mr Blackwood.

Mr and Mrs Blackwood walked away.

"We need to find a way out of here," said Ivory.

"There's a key hanging right outside the cell!" exclaimed Mateo.

"Whose hand would even fit through that?" asked Ivory.

Everyone looked at her.

"Great," she muttered.

She stuck her hand out and tried to grab the key.

"Ivory, you're almost there," said Avery.

"Yeah, just a little bit closer!" said Julianna.

She yelped as she drew her hand back.

"What's wrong now?" asked Randy, annoyed.

"I think I cut myself," said Ivory, "but I'm fine." She stuck her hand out again and her fingers brushed against the key. She finally grasped it.

"Got it!"

"Now unlock the damn cell!" said Randy.

She twisted the key, and the door opened.

"Come on, let's stop them," I said.

We all ran and then Blaire saw something.

"What's that?" she asked.

We all turned to find a big red button that said,

'TURN POWERS ON.'

We pressed the button as quickly as possible and ran to the room labelled

'MR. BLACKWOOD'S BIG PROJECT ROOM KEEP OUT!'

We saw a big bucket and a cannon machine.

"He's going to launch the substance into the air!" exclaimed Randy.

The bucket was labelled R.A.D. It stood for Radioactive Acidic Distillate.

The smell was sharp, chemical, wrong. Ivory gagged.

Julianna whispered, "That's what we saw at the factory..."

"What do we do with it?" asked Avery.

"Mateo, try to burn it," I said.

"I don't think I should," said Mateo, pointing to the 'Flammable' sign on the bucket.

"I know what to do," said Randy.

"What?" I asked.

"Let's throw it on Mr Blackwood and Mrs Lindsey," said Randy darkly.

"I guess that could work," I said.

"We need to create a distraction," said Julianna.

"I'll make the bucket float and pour on his head," said Randy.

"I'll stop him at the perfect time with my mind," I said.

"I'll tangle them up in ivy," said Ivory.

"I'll stop them from thinking," said Avery.

"My power is luck," said Blaire.

"Okay, then stay here and hope for the best," I said.

"By the way, my codename is Brantor," said Blake.

"Mine's Luxen," said Blaire.

"I can distract them," said Julianna.

"Same," said Mateo.

"Me too," said Blake.

"Okay, let's do this," I said.

"Hands in everyone!" said Julianna.

We all put our hands together.

"Three, two, one, team go!" We all said in unison.

"Brantor, Sorren, Oceria go!" I yelled.

Blake, Mateo and Julianna ran to the front of the building where Mr and Mrs Blackwood were.

"Hey, how did you get out of the cell?" shouted Mr Blackwood.

Everybody started running, using their powers to confuse the Blackwoods.

"Oceria, ready?" asked Mateo.

"Ready if you are, Sorren!" said Julianna.

They both smiled and nodded.

Mateo shot fire out and Julianna shot water at it. They balanced it perfectly, making smoke. They ran while making the smoke.

"Operation Smokescreen is initiating," said Mateo, as if he were a robot.

"That was the surprise!" exclaimed Julianna.

We stared at it in awe. It must've taken a long time to practice and balance their powers perfectly.

Mr and Mrs Blackwood looked around, confused. Mateo and Julianna stopped the smokescreen.

"Seraphyll, Cerephiel now!" I yelled.

Avery used his powers to stop them from thinking. Mr and Mrs Blackwood clutched their heads in pain while Ivory tied them up, hanging upside down.

"Make it stop!" yelled Mr Blackwood.

"Nyxia, Levark now!" shouted Julianna.

I made sure that Mr Blackwood stayed still while Randy poured the R.A.D. on both of their heads. They evaporated into thin air.

"We actually did it!" I exclaimed.

We all started screaming with joy and hugged each other.

"We saved the world!" exclaimed Randy.

Suddenly a sharp voice rang through our ears. "That was only phase one."

We turned to Avery.

"That wasn't me," he said.

"Maybe you projected it by accident," said Randy.

"Maybe," whispered Avery.

The rest of the school year was pretty boring. Blaire wasn't *as* rude to us because we were the only ones who understood her. Her minions all thought she was crazy, but she still hangs out with them. What we did made the news, and we told them everything except for us having superpowers. Our teachers and principal Davis didn't give us detention for the rest of the year because of that. We won a trophy for saving our country and the world.

We still train every day near my locker. We didn't have to have an assessment for History because the only reason we had to do it was because of Mr Blackwood's plan.

Epilogue

11:57 pm 31st December 1984

We went to a new pizza shop with an amazing sky view to celebrate everything that happened that year. The whole shop was lit up in neon pinks and blues. A couple of arcade machines were lined up in the corner, humming. The city was glowing with Christmas lights that hadn't been taken down and people with glowing bracelets and necklaces filling the streets to see the fireworks.

Grease stained our fingers and every time I brought my fizzy drink near my mouth my nose tickled. The pizza was oily but not disgustingly oily, so I was fine with it.

Mateo groaned, glancing at the arcade machines. "If I had one more quarter, I'd totally beat my Pac-Man record."

Avery rolled his eyes, but still dug into his pocket like he might hand one over. The shop started playing music faintly, like it was the end of a movie.

"This was a really good year," I said, lifting up my cheesy pizza.

"Yeah, I actually had so much fun with you guys!" Julianna beamed, raising her glass to the middle of the table.

"Yeah, same," said Mateo raising his glass.

"Me too," said Ivory as she slid her glass forward.

"Same," said Avery nudging his glass in.

I smiled and added mine to the pile. "Me as well."

Randy adjusted his glasses, still holding his ever-present Rubik's Cube in one hand, but with the other he tapped his soda can into the centre. "Alright, alright, fine. Same here."

We all leaned in, hands brushing as the glasses and cans touched. Our little mismatched group. Our family.

"Three... two... one..."

"Cheers and happy New Year!" we all shouted, laughing as we clinked our glasses.

Fireworks exploded outside, brighter now, painting the sky in red, green and gold. Julianna tilted her head back to watch them, her eyes wide like a little kid's. Ivory leaned against Avery's shoulder, fiddling with her necklace. Mateo tried to flip a pizza crust into his mouth, missed spectacularly, and groaned as it smacked the floor, making us all laugh harder. Even Randy cracked a grin.

For the first time in a long time, there was no fighting, no teachers, no detentions, no powers to hide.

Just us. Friends.

"Next year's gonna be even better," Julianna said, and for the first time, I believed her.

Teaser

" Today on Ravenwood news. Police have arrested a girl. She showed signs of radiation when a police officer pulled her over because she looked 'odd'. The scientists have done many tests on her, and they found out that she has superhuman abilities. The term people are calling these things are *Variants*. She is now unconscious, and the police have taken her in as a prisoner."

– Operation R.A.D. II
Coming soon

Author's note

This book was written for anyone who's ever felt different. Operation R.A.D. started as a story about a group of friends and a trip gone wrong and became a story about courage, trust, fear, what it means to be a teenager and what happens when ordinary people end up in extraordinary danger.

If you've ever felt like you don't fit in, you were never meant to.
– Maya Ahmed

Acknowledgements

Writing this novel has been so much fun I thank

My parents, who encouraged me to do what I love most.

My sister who made inside jokes with me about the book when I had writer's block.

www.ingramcontent.com/pod-product-compliance
Lightning Source LLC
Chambersburg PA
CBHW032007180726
48283CB00008B/2584